PRAISE FOR
ANSGAR ALLEN

"Allen has distilled the speculations of Nietzsche and Freud into an impersonal meatspace whose soulless protagonist is writing its own suicide note – while time dissolves all, while the space of inscription reveals caverns measureless to man. *Black Vellum* is the work of an extremely subtle mind, co-opting horror to trace the integuments of a glitching futurity somehow liberated from the traditional impasses of nihilism." –David Roden, author of *Snuff Memories*

"The intellect was only first produced as a result of this diminishment of perception, writes Ansgar Allen in *Black Vellum*. This is an exquisitely written philosophical tale about human civilization as the quest for order, measurement, and automation—and perhaps, about how nihilism and despair have always fed our fantasies of humanoid machines."
— Germán Sierra, author of *The Artifact*

"Ansgar Allen has quickly become one of my favorite authors. He takes risks and writes well—these things alone are a rarity today. Equal parts informative, entertaining, and aesthetically appealing, *Plague Theatre* is an excellent introduction to his evolving oeuvre."
— D. Harlan Wilson, author of *The Psychotic Dr. Schreber*

"*The Wake and the Manuscript* is an involving book, a textual persistence relentless in its chapter-less, paragraph-free form, start to finish. The story is a captivating oddity, a monolithic confession or lamentation, an existential interrogation inhabited with flashbacks, foibles, sickness, death, hallucination, mental aberration, religion and belief [...] exquisitely weird."
—Eugen Bacon, *AUREALIS MAGAZINE*

THE FACES OF PLUTO
Copyright © 2024 Ansgar Allen
ISBN: 978-1-960451-08-8

ANSGAR ALLEN

THE FACES OF PLUTO

STALKING HORSE PRESS
SANTA FE, NEW MEXICO

THE FACES OF PLUTO

We cannot hope to live so long in our names, as some have done in their persons… 'Tis too late to be ambitious. The great mutations of the world are acted.

Thomas Browne

Rhythm is originally the rhythm of the feet. All animals that walk will make it. Only humans take note, paying attention for their own half steps and the steps of others. No gait is regular or perfectly repeated and nothing is set to stay as it is. *Man has always listened to the footsteps of other men,* and the brutes.

—hoofed animals flee in herds, like regiments of drummers. The first musical notations were read in animal tracks. Little toes— minor notes. The bigger ones—flick and fall, longest traces in sand. Some kind of origin of words here too, there, where, or about which they learned to read.

The locusts' wings say 'throng, throng'; Well may your sons and grandsons be a host innumerable. Their endless line an open and unfinished grave. But chance a look upward too, for they *ought to know that the space between heaven and earth is not empty,* and as a consequence most ages, but *the Christian Middle Ages* worst of all, *gave serious thought to the number of devils* that flew from one side to another, mingling in swarms. If a legion of daemons can enter a man, how many can drive a kingdom, or cause the pious to itch in their beds. Bit by invisible crowds they got up and wandered, their feet still treading lines of script.

§

About the recessed doorway the sides lean inward. It resembles those unearthed in Eastern Europe opening to Mesolithic burial chambers.

—in a late century study, *Doorways of Primitives*, the trapezoid is considered intermediate between the archway and the doorway properly speaking. It is written, moreover, that the slanting shape signifies indecision, or more favourably, a suspicion of the vertical, or of lines which point equally to the heavens as they do to the depths.

§

The door opens to a space neither within the wall nor beyond it. Which can only mean, no matter how far gone inwards there is no way of seeing the wall from the inside. In the lintel is a five-word inscription, its words unmistakable despite their erosion. The form, which is archaic, can for the most part be read by the deeper cuts.

—*the bowels of a letter* are more determinate than the instrokes, the outstrokes, even the spurs. In the letter b, for instance, there is the instroke at the base and the ascender that points north. Each would have given outwards an additional flourish, then eroded, and gone. And so, something like *b*, becomes *b*, and with further erosion reduces to a letter resembling an oblate sphere—*the sign of a rotating planet*—but never perfectly o, and with further spalling becomes the letter c but turned, so once again not perfectly of the letter.

—*the various winds* and rains and frosts can only approximate the act of writing. In any case, it cannot be presumed that the script of the lintel was Latinate, making these speculations on letter cutting and letter erosion somewhat redundant. It cannot be said either that the characters were rounded, and that the shift from papyrus to vellum had occurred, which is to say, the transition from rough surfaces favouring multiple-stroke orthographies, to smooth materials favouring single-stroke letters and those parts of the grapheme known as *embowelments*.

§

In the yet-to-be-fully catalogued assets of the British Museum there is a tablet with cuneiform inscription about which its discoverer and transporter wrote, *I have seen Latin here, and Greek, and Arabic.* The wedges are cut from more than one angle and appear to be mutually hostile. To a military eye they resemble the arrows of units engaged in battle or heading to some future annihilation. In actual fact, the cuneiform wedge recalls the flight pattern of the stork, and so the script itself, which might be one of the earliest examples of true writing, would first appear in the sky.

§

It is said the first monk killed by raiders at Lindisfarne had just finished scribing the letter b. It would be too neat if the word aimed for was Beelzebub, and so was written *Beelzeb~*, or perhaps even *Beelzebub~*. Those who knew to rumour well would never claim it so. Surviving monks of other coast monasteries did report similar instances of the last letter written by the first slain. Which is why manuscripts of this period, and

11

region, are occasionally found containing a form of constrained writing that omits the letter b. There is mention of a complete text of the vulgate bible that was produced under this restriction.

The technical term for it was *the castrated vulgate.* Some have taken this titular sign through its end to suggest this was not constrained but *castrated* writing. Which implies a different origin. The little menfolk—as the Norsemen saw them—did not so much write the compacted vulgate from fear of the letter as they did from lack of ardour. Writing for these monks had once been an act of blinding love, the sublimation of testicular attention. Those who lost their ardour produced damaged and unlovable bibles which reflected, so they felt, their own condition before God.

§

Various pedants have observed that lowercase script was not yet in use when Lindisfarne was raided. This would mean the letter *b* would have been more like *B*, so there was no ascender pointing north. This, more likely, was the orthographic context in which the first monk was killed in the scriptorium. Other pedants subsequently pointed out how ascenders were still present but launched differently. Some of these tended to point northeast, which was more accurate as a portent. Still others have weighed in—such is the thrall of disagreement—and objected to cartographic reading in the first place, and have suggested situated reading instead, so that ascenders point to the roof and descenders into the lap and groin of the monk where the ink was occasionally flicked.

It is also claimed that the first monk killed by heathen raiders lost half his skull to the axe, and that the word *migraine*, a deliberate corruption of the Greek term for 'half-skull', was derived from this moment, and was used by monks subsequently to describe the effect of too much writing.

A standing joke between monks at Lindisfarne—they would tell it when standing, that is to say, when taking a break from scribing—was to recall how the Greeks considered the coastline to be a sort of trough out of which you must travel by climbing or sailing to the higher parts of the world. Others described the coast, this trench, as a very long grave. So much for the monks at Lindisfarne.

§

The words of the lintel are presented as a riddle, and this alone indicates their age. Oracles and diviners are so long dead, the humble riddle—their last residue—has come into disuse. Those wishing to be admitted, which is to say, those wishing to admit themselves, will come under the inscription and find their transit deferred by the contents of the wall. That is, they will come upon mile upon mile of books. This is not a pleasant discovery, something so-called bookish people may struggle to understand.

§

—I do think that we largely delude ourselves with the knowledge that we think we possess, that we make it up as we go along, that we make it fit our desires and anxieties and that we invent a straight line of a trail in order to calm ourselves down—

§

Every book carries with it a version of the pain it may produce, or has the capacity for, as well as the many names under which pain is misrecognised as pleasure.

§

The so-called pleasures of reading are over-stated and generally thought about when not reading.

§

The worst book from a reader's perspective is not the worst book a reader can identify.

§

The worst book is undecided in its nature and will not let a reader settle into one or other habit of reading and habit of judgement.

§

A book can never be undecided in its nature. There is no indecision in a book. If indecision ever existed, it is long dead by the production of the book.

§

Books are produced with their crimes baked in. The book which mixes the so-called crime of falsehood with the pain of truth and adds to these the mischief of not marking within its pages the transition from one to the other.

Or the book which takes within itself an antique idiom, as if its author had learned nothing from all attempts to break from that idiom, and yet which admits a voice by way of it, a manner of describing, perhaps even seeing, by an act of displaced ventriloquism, a borrowed voice ushered from a destroyed past to a desolate present. So much for books.

There is a man beyond the woods, he requires a replacement. This one will be able to read and be willing to come, it read. Or must think himself willing as if he willed it, was added. The note is specific on that, its handler went on. It could be for nobody else.

These were not his words, but they were evident by its thrusting. Either way, the carrier had in mind to give me the note. He would spend no time finding others to receive it. Most decisive acts reach the point of decision in this way, as signs of exhaustion, conclusions to the boredom of deciding.

My receiving of the note surprised me little. My being its recipient, its only receiver, could be made to make sense. Few living there where I was ever left, and fewer still could be imagined leaving now. I require an assistant, it goes on, any person will do, so long as they can read, and so long as they can write.

Knowing how reading is no simple matter, and writing is nothing but the exactitude of pain, I was equally unstruck to find the specification narrowed further. This person must be conversant with various understandings, it continued. And should have canny powers of inscription and recollection. The candidate must both inscribe and recollect, it clarified, where each recollection must be an inscription, and each inscription a recollection. Thinking myself literate, it would be senseless to think otherwise, and knowing myself to be well studied—having learnt the art of inscription and of recollection in my youth—I knew again the handler was right and I was its rightful receiver.

Some sort of cart or carriage must be found, I decided, a vehicle that does not need to be returned. I shall take the thing and travel with it to find the author of this request. That was how I went about it in the quarry which was also a town, asking for a cart but finding every cart in use. Each was loaded with rock or otherwise encumbered. Even empty carts when approached seemed to fill if only with the owner's intentions. They saw me come and as I approached began looking for something that needed loading. Load me up instead, is what I might have said.

In this quest of mine the handler of the note was sure to be of no use. He did not even reply to my requests to refuse them. I will need a cart, I said. Or was it, well find me a cart. Or even the more direct and reasonable request that the handler himself lend me the cart he had come in upon, and which stood right by him as he passed me the note. This two-wheeled trap was good enough for the job. I will take your two-wheeled trap, said I as he led it off and away. Your two-wheeled trap will serve me well, I repeated as the trap grew smaller. It served the handler of the note to make it here and would surely serve me in returning there. The pony, moreover, might have some memory of the route through the forest and would know better where we must travel to.

§

Having walked only to clear my head of those things that accumulate and clutter the mind of every thinking and non-thinking person, it was my misfortune—there is no other word—to encounter the gentleman, fully clothed and half submerged in a hollow. With one hand he held a book by

Thomas Browne from which he quoted.

—men have been most phantasticall in the singular contrivances of their corporall dissolution—

And in the other a collection of Jorge Louis Borges' writings stained all through. He said no other method but of melodrama would do, and every burial mound testifies to human melodrama, and only the soberest people bury their dead without ornament, and only by conjuring a similar though not identical sentiment of excessive drama in himself would he ever understand why it was that past civilizations had left so many barrows for him to excavate.

The half-submerged man said this to me from the hollow, his excavated hole, and reached out a long arm, intolerably elongated, and clawed another fistful of earth to cover himself with, then launched into a series of complaints levelled against that inveterate barrow digger, his peer the Englishman, who took his own dissatisfaction at one dig to his digging of the next. This Englishman is the author of the widely unknown book, *Ten Years' Diggings in Celtic and Saxon Grave Hills.* The period covered by *Ten Years' Diggings* is the shunted decade 1848 to 1858. Our meeting at the hollow could not have been before 1861, which is when his barrow-obsessed peer was himself buried, or so the man in the hollow had me recall.

It must have been in the region of 1861, or just thereafter, that I met him in his hollow, I thought, bemoaning as he lay half-submerged this Thomas Bateman and Bateman's *Ten Years' Digging.* As he clawed the earth, he lamented it, and his laments propelled the clawing, the combined effect of which sounded like –f –f –f –f –f –f –f –f.

§

Bateman's own tomb was subsequently listed. This occurred in 1967. That is to say, over a hundred years later. As a grade II listed building Bateman's tomb *warrants every effort to preserve it.* Buildings in this category cannot be altered, or indeed extended, without special planning permission.

§

Section of Parcelly Hay Barrow.

Bateman's son did not share his father's passion. Every time father says barrow, I hear burrow, wrote the son in his diary. And I would rather a burrow any day.

The son was tormented mercilessly by his peers for being the scion of a barrow digger, and then, inexplicably, for also being the progeny of the notorious Mary Bateman of Leeds and not the son of Sarah Bateman, née Sarah Parker, his actual mother, even though the dates did not stack up at all, not even remotely. Mary of Leeds would have been his grandmother, if that, her execution having been of the year 1809. This fact notwithstanding, the local youth made a habit of leaving eggs about for the barrow digger's son to find, on each of which was written, CRIST IS COMING, or alternately CHRIST IS COMING, all of it after the egg that Mary Bateman said she herself did once find laid by her very own hen. Or they would come at him with leather bound books and say it was the skin of the mother, this being also grounded in a truth of sorts, given that two books were indeed commissioned of Mary's hide, and strips of it sold as charms or curiosities—'tis true, as the children would say, or something of the sort. There was a good trade in criminal offcuts about this time. The tip of her tongue came into the possession of the governor of the local gaol, although what he did with it later is not known. This tip survived in a pickle jar till the 1950s, after which, and much disintegrated, it was thought best disposed of. So much for Mary Bateman.

I can see you with your pen, the man said from his hollow. There was no pen in my hand, but I took his point. You will falsify all this with *circumstantial details*, he said, quoting Borges, by a habit *which contaminates everything with falsity, since those details can abound in the realities but not in their recollection.* To which I replied that in his case inscription preceded recollection, which meant that all details, even the most essential such as his being in a hole, were falsehoods, essentially. For me to note circumstantial details surrounding his being in a hole, of how his hair was matted, and his beard too, and that it reminded me of the matted hair of a felled and dampened beast, could hardly make matters worse. To which he replied with the words of the lintel.

I said nothing, even though the point of the riddle, so I felt, was to collapse its terms and remain at ease in the context of their destruction.

I did not add, either, that the book-filled here of the there of the wall contains all known ideas, taken to include all ideas that have been had but which have not been made known, and certainly all that have been inscribed, including the very notion of absolute inscription—another impossible fancy. This form of writing, better described as a type of action, or more simply, as a trace-giving gesture, produces the trace which precedes the gesture. It must project its language and the language of its values in the very novelty of each mark, or effect.

His point nonetheless stood about the smallest details in fiction, those intended to conjure a reality effect. These are the most compressed form of a lie. This lie, the lie of the conventional novel in particular, is meant to conceal the irreality of fiction, or throw a gentle veil about it, even though the irreality of fiction is surely the most alluring, and the truest, if not also the most unattainable of its promises.

§

§

Along the prints of a retreating horse I came upon a man in shallow pit who said—most of us are remembered in the shadiest of details. A life is encapsulated and so ruined in that circumstantial detail—*remember how such and such had that thing about… remember how they said that about this, and that about that, and how they thought this or that was a sign of decadence,* and so on. I shall be remembered differently, said he, for digging and living in this hole.

§

Following the rumours uphill, I found a man submerged to the waist by his own doing. In one hand a copy of Browne's HYDRIOTAPHIA, URNE BURIALL, OR, *Discourse of the Sepulchrall Urnes lately found in* NORFOLK—with which he gestured—and then, by way of that movement of hand and book, beat a long invective against his peer, the Englishman, Thomas Bateman, who went from one barrow to the next, driven by the emptiness of his country mansion and the parlour-like vapidity of his soul, each not yet full enough with human detritus.

Quoting Browne somewhat against Browne's intentions, I thought, the man in the hollow said, IT WILL NOT DO to *mercifully preserve their bones, and pisse not upon their ashes.*

The entire lot of exhumation and preservation of artefacts is surely absurd, he said, if not pointlessly indulgent, when we are surrounded by so much inhumation and rot. It would be better to practice a bit of inhumation on our own selves, said he, and experience some measure of rot, if we are to learn something worth knowing about our predicament.

His pursuit was not Browne's, so he said, and he did not, like Browne, believe *all customs were founded upon some bottome of Reason.*

This gave Browne license to speculate a fair bit upon one thing or another, including an early argument for burial and against cremation.

—being of the opinion *that water was the originall of all things,* Thales *thought it most equall to submit unto the principle of putrefaction, and conclude in a moist relentment,* writes Browne.

Or in plainer language, if the world first emerged from a swamp-like environment, it seems more fitting to bury the dead in the damp earth and let the bodies liquefy than burn them, which would be against nature, or at least against reason.

The man in his hollow—who was, incidentally, sporting a long and matted beard—had little time for such speculations much as he enjoyed Browne as a writer. From a poetic aspect, so he said, Browne was perfectly bearable. From a reasoning aspect, he was objectionable. Browne is still worth reading from a reasoning aspect, the man in the hollow went on, but only if the reader is reminded at every line that Browne understood reason in its locale. Browne saw how every given reason is locally produced, and so reason in general must be treated with caution. Reason will always have its own specifics. This, at least, was the gist of what the man said in his hole.

Seeing reason this way, that is to say, viewing reason as a local thing whilst cleaving to reason as a general concept, allows Browne to perform a double manoeuvre. It might be described as the saving flaw of his humanism, or its principle of restraint. For Browne will at once observe how *men have lost their reason in nothing so much as their religion, wherein stones and clouts make martyrs*—and so can deplore those who have lost their reason in the general sense—but then Browne will also say, *since the religion of one seems madnesse unto another, to afford an account or rationall of old Rites requires no rigid Reader*—

The reason of others must needs be understood by flexing and elasticating one's own. If we are to understand Thales, for instance, said the man in the hole, we must place the reasoning of Thales in its context. The worst mistake we can make, the man continued, is to call Thales the first philosopher and make him stand for reason because of it.

I stood and listened to all this as the man in his hollow repeatedly raised one arm, the arm without a book, and lifted it over the rim to claw back clods of earth.

Walking back away I turned and shouted at him there clawing—*but what of Thales predicting an eclipse.*

To which the man scarcely faltered at the rim and said, *yes, the Greeks were crafty in their wisdom. Is it not the case that Anaxagoras predicted a meteorite.*

§

She led me by the hand until we reached the brow of the hill and then, with a nod, indicated the barrow in its leeward bank. As we drew close, I saw beside the barrow was dug a shallow depression in which lay a man with matted hair. With one hand he held a book by Thomas Browne, the other was stained by earth beat under the fingernails to horizons.

To subsist in lasting Monuments, to live in their productions, he began saying, quoting Browne, but then broke off at the sight of my recognition. Looking me closely, he motioned his lips, a gesture to gather time with.

And if any have been so happy as truly to understand Christian annihilation, extasis, exolution, liquefaction, said he with a pause, and *gustation of God,* another pause, which grew, and became convulsive once again with the whetting of his lips. Raising himself on an elbow, a gesture which may be mistaken as the sign of the soul becoming erect, the man in the hollow by the barrow said, with more definite intent—

But man is a Noble Animal, splendid in ashes, and pompous in the grave.

By the time I turned from his pit, the girl, who had taken me this far, was bounding in short but certain steps around the circumference of the hill, losing height and fleeing us both so long as I could see about its edge and after which we were alone, myself, the barrow, and him.

Some while later, after I had left the barrow, the hollow, and its troglodyte—I would call him that—and had been wandering in the valley below wondering what to do with what I had learned of his excavations, I did meet again the girl who led me there but subsequently fled. She was sat by a well, gazing downward from its rim. In response to my question about her fleeing it appeared that she, too, was able to quote Thomas Browne verbatim, for she said without reflection—

It was tedious leading you to him for sure, *but the most tedious being is that which can unwish itself, content to be nothing.*

Unheeding this remark, and more stimulated by the fact of its making, I set upon my interrogations of the girl, asking where she was taught the line, who had instructed her to repeat it, and whether this person was the very same hollow dweller up on the hill. She made as if to leave, unencumbered, as little children can be, by the hold of my questioning, and so I gripped her by the arm and repeated my statements as to her instruction. This caused her to shrivel and grow old in my grasp, nearing that nothing which moments before seemed a lifetime away, and from a mouth puckered by age to resemble the nether orifice, she spoke words which now seemed more befitting of their host—

Oblivion is not to be hired, said she, once more quoting Browne.

This sight did not strike me as odd or surprising. It is a scene I have seen many times before.

§

See upon my face the charter of all faces, said she, *for as from our beginning we run through a variety of Looks before we come to consistent and settled Faces; so before our End, by sick and languishing Alterations, we put on new Visages.*

Or so wrote Browne of someone he saw grow old before his time and die of it.

§

She arrived to the surface sat upon a bucket, gazing at the winch he was winding, and said, *the world is a place not to live but to die in.* He asked her if she was not the same person just seen grow old and fall backwards into the well. She said he looked small, that he was a dot against the sky, and now he had raised her above ground, he was not a dot, but a hole.

In his thinking and writing, he might have replied, *he sought to look upon earthly existence, from the things that were closest to him to the spheres of the universe, with the eye of an outsider, one might even say of the creator.*

Or so writes Sebald, of Browne.

§

Browne ranges no higher than an insect and has a similar temper.

—he ranges like a bee over the whole variegated garden of contemporary thought, sipping where he will, integrating what he needs into his own personal, creative interpretation of the universe, writes somebody else.

This somebody else wrote fifty years before Sebald, and nobody knows his name.

§

Browne places himself not among the insects, but among the frogs and the newts and the toads.

—we are onely that amphibious piece between a corporal and spiritual Essence, writes he.

Which makes Browne and every other of his kind a *middle form,* a creature living between two realms with no secure knowledge or base in either.

—thus is Man that great and true Amphibium, whose nature is disposed to live, not onely like other creatures in diverse elements, but in divided and distinguished worlds.

§

The writer does not loom above the text as a supreme adjudicator, or all-seeing eye, but performs distance as an expression of human limitation, said he.

§

This writer writes with the eye of an outsider, perhaps even of the creator, when failing to stand outside, or truly create.

§

The writer lays wet ink on a dry page, and only exists as a writer so long as the former glistens.

§

The writer makes a virtue of divergent and distracted reading, writes the writer. So much for the writer.

§

If nothing can be fully known, the intellect finds no secure home, no place of comfort, and sees that it is entitled to none—nothing that is cosy, or close, or which conveys a feeling of security by its proximity. In this respect the intellect bears analogy to a mote, a flake of barely lit ash struck by a breeze into the upper atmosphere.

§

When Browne sets down his prose with a contrived authorial distance, this is a symptom of the imperfection of his learning. Detachment as the sign of an unseated, uneasy intellect.

§

Few writers of his distinction have shown less professional interest in literature as such, writes that same somebody else of Browne— and this saved him from many of its vices, that same somebody else adds. Browne never wrote as artist alone; he sought something beyond the mere ornament of the word and used language to raise himself to it.

§

Browne took some interest in food, and mentions venison most often in his letters as if he had a special taste for it. His diet was fairly broad, and the man did once eat dolphin but drew the line at the lower colon.

—There is a dayntie bitt accounted by many, called the Inspinne. The dish is made of the *Intestinum Rectum* of a deer, writes Browne, otherwise known as the straight intestine, or the last short passage before the anal canal. I know of no other animal *wherein the Rectum is cooked up.* The piece is turned inside outward and is broiled and fried and much desired by some. I have seen it myself at gentleman's tables, *butt my stomack went agaynst it.*

§

The word *Inspinne* has seen little usage in the English language beyond Browne relating a rectal delicacy. It is likely nobody knows of any other instance.

§

In a subsequent century the word *Inspinne* might be confused with the Norwegian term *Ispinne,* meaning *popsicle stick* or *lollipop.*

§

Browne was able to combine an interest in all things including the rectal delicacy with being a doctor. This amounted, in large part, to offering remedies and prescriptions that were more or less useless. And then recording the details of their failure.

—Our Deane after a languishing sickness of about 2 yeares left this world early on thursday morning. Hee voyded for a long time many small stones, much gravell, & often of late much blood, together with the very parenchyma of his left kidney.

§

As a doctor, Browne had the authority to sentence the dying, or let the dying know of their sentence, and came up with all manner of strange ways of expressing it.

—Upon my first Visit I was bold to tell them who had not let fall all hopes for his Recovery, That in my sad Opinion he was not like to behold a Grashopper, much less to pluck another Fig.

§

Having seen more of dying than most people, Browne said he knew how death was typically no easy thing, and how it involved some kind of eruption in the fabric of being that the being struggled to cross.

—With what strife and pains we came into the World we know not; but 'tis commonly no easie matter to get out of it.

This judgement allowed Browne to remark of a few of his patients how theirs was uncommonly easy—*his Departure was so easie*—and so present the idea of an undemanding death, a death the dying could not complain of. Elsewhere Browne describes this death he once witnessed as, *his soft Departure* and *his soft Death,* the dying man himself here remaining anonymous. The young adult who died so softly, whose departure was so easie, was reduced to nearly half himself, Browne adds, and left off thereby a great part of himself which need not be carried to the grave. The two lobes of his lungs were adhered to the side and his living flesh was so thin the anatomy of the gut could be read from without—*an Aruspex might have read a Lecture on him without Exenteration,* writes Browne, referring here to that ancient species of priest more usually found divining from the entrails of animals.

—these details may be found in Browne's *Letter to a Friend,* one of his other compositions in fine English style which Browne would be celebrated for.

Which all of it considered was how the Doctor still stood himself above all dying, and all death, in the fullness of his erudition.

§

Browne was a writer of sick notes, and might be one of the pioneer practitioners of this noble art.

—*I humbly certifie that the Right Reverend Father in god Anthonie Lord Bishop of Norwich is and hath been long afflicted with the stone and paynfull diseases of the bladder and urinarie parts that hee is not possibly able to endure the motion of a coach for a few miles and upon every attempt to go abroad in his coach makes bloody urine & is much payned after, so that it may hazard his life to undertake a London Journey.*

§

Being a doctor amounted in no small part to having the words to describe his own ailments too and complain with the force of being right in his assessment at the effects of his work.

*—Extraordinarie sickly seasons woorie physitians, & robbeth them
of their health as well as their quiet,* so take care of your own
health, and be mindful, Browne writes his son, because there
is a sick season now upon us.

§

Browne's first born was a doctor like his father. The father
would write numerous letters to his son outlining how exactly
he purged and vomited his latest patients—which concoctions
he made and how—and which patients were not so much in
need of purging and vomiting but might benefit from a little
bloodletting instead.

§

Not every vomiting fit Browne sees fit to mention was of his own
doing. Occasionally people vomited without him. *I remember a
woeman,* Browne writes his son, *who being thirstie in a quartan
ague, called for a bottle of beere, butt the servant in hast brought her
a bottle of Inck,* which she drank a goodly amount of *& vomitted
much and black.* Curiously, the fever left her, and she was cured.

§

Mr. Wisse is a tolerable man. Unwilling to offend God or cause
a disturbance in the fabrick of his outlook, he does not trouble
himself with perplexing thoughts. But I perceived his head to
be busy five or six days ago, *so hee was lett blood & tooke his usual
purge.* The man came again yesterday regarding his head, but
it is not his head but his nether which bothers him truly, since

he hath a Tumor in scrotio. He will not let me look at it, *though it is now so bigge that it can not easily bee concealed.* Perhaps he will be willing to let you have sight of it when he next visits London, writes Browne to his son.

Mr. Hayset, or it might be Hasset, will most likely visit you, and I would have you view his penis most diligently, for *he say he have some gleeting at the tip of it,* and at times this gleeting is not simply some but of a great amount, and there is trouble too with the erection. I gave him some mercurial medicines and decoctions and he said it grew well, but that he is still not free of the gleeting. Please do employ the utmost secrecy. The man is soon to be married to a great gentlewoman, or this is what he intends, and it is only fit that he should be in a state of body that will be *safe and congruus unto both.* He hath moreover a pretty good estate and is not unlikely to be ungrateful.

A gentlewoman with a prolapsed uterus is on her way to Bath via London, writes Browne to his son, and I fear *shee may be disordered by the tumbling & jouncing* of her journey. Might you know of someone who makes corks covered with wax which are used in cases such as these, and might you also be able to recommend the best coach to take from London to Bath, he asks his son, which is to say, a coach with not so much tumbling and jouncing as the gentlewoman will have suffered on the journey from Norwich to London. I heard of a woman who went two years ago to Bath and she was cured of something similar. For my part I did manage to offer some purging drinks, but she said it made things come down all the more. So to Bath, I said, and this is now her predicament.

§

Browne appears to have spent as much if not most of his time not producing works of literary distinction but engaged in the activity of doctoring. He spent a fair amount of time cutting up animals too, and writing his son about which animals he had lately taken apart, and then again what was the latest concoction for inducing a purge.

§

—*His only means of achieving the sublime heights that his endeavour required was a parlous loftiness in his language,* writes Sebald of Browne.

Sebald has in mind the side-endeavour of producing those works that Browne would become famous for, but which occupied so little of his time comparative to the purging and the writing about purging, and the cutting up of animals.

In this literary side-endeavour, Browne relied upon the fullness of his erudition, even as it never sufficed. In those pieces Browne was carried off by the structures of his prose *constructing labyrinthine sentences that sometimes extend over one or two pages, sentences that resemble processions or a funeral cortège in their sheer ceremonial lavishness.*

Sebald does not suggest whose funeral this is, though it is tempting to see Browne acting out the coming death of his own specific breed of writing, leaving others to subsequently, and somewhat mournfully remark, Browne remains unmatched as a prose stylist.

—because of the immense weight of the impediments he is carrying, Browne's writing can be held back by the force of gravitation, Sebald himself goes on, *but when he does succeed in rising higher and higher through the circles of his spiralling prose, borne aloft like a glider on warm currents of air, even today the reader is overcome by a sense of levitation.*

The world is placed under fragile inspection—fragile because lightly built, gossamer thin—and viewed from extraordinary distances, then held close again and to the light.

And yet, says Browne, all knowledge is enveloped in darkness. What we perceive are no more than isolated lights in the abyss of ignorance, in the shadow-filled edifice of the world. We study the order of things, says Browne, but we cannot grasp their innermost essence. And because it is so, it befits our philosophy to be writ small.

§

When Browne looked into the nether regions of his patients, he also reported it to be dark, entirely dark, which accounted for the drawing out of their contents—to bring forth something from that darkness, and so too for the cutting up of animals—to turn bodies out of themselves and open their innards to the light.

Having walked and read and lived out his sense of the outside, he made it to the wall and its book-filled recesses. I have come to see the act of reading in all its duplicity, said he. Worst of all the reader who holds each book overlong and learns what is held by heart. This for the notion that with words etched in the brain, or the mind's eye, a reader will always have the materials of escape already absorbed, even if the entirety of it were combusted, or the walls fell inward, or, less drastically, even if confined to a cell, or simply found alone and facing a moment of solitude with nothing no book to grasp at, no conversation to hold at the ear, these words, once loved, whichever words they were will return, for none would be able to rob them of it. This is their fancy.

Or those who read to contribute something lasting of their own, something worth leaving. The word *worth* carries rake lines that would parse the future in preparation if they could—*the future as a gracious receiver*—

And so too readers who can be seen to stray but in glazing over do not escape. Their inattention is a further sign of their enslavement—*the idiocy of holding a book that is not doing its work on the mind*—

A more helpful inscription on the lintel outside would be along these lines or a substrate of them—

WITH MY INSCRIPTION replacing that which currently exists, those who enter would be confronted by the imaginary of this space and know outright to take all imaginaries lightly. This was the edict before all visitors, to exceed its books, even if so many seem to have failed in their advance, and never venture further than the initial chambers, antechambers, and the first passages. The internal walls cannot breathe, and so they moulder. Every chamber, no matter its width, is broken by twin lines of shelves backed to each other, all spaces filled with their rows, cut by lines transverse. Not a modest doorway lacking a shelf or two under which the wanderer must pass—a yearnful image, perhaps, but to those who walk it, soon a torment. Many consider themselves artful in their readings and hold each book and read it artful-like. They sit and take their books figuratively, or earnestly, it hardly matters which. For even the artful among them have never exceeded this region and gone through. The inner door is of the same proportions as the outer one, and has the very same lintel, only its lintel is blank. The inner door is also devoid of any kind of furniture, or fixings, or indentations, or texture. I have long considered passing back out through the outer doorway to chisel those words, my preferred words. Those passing under would be fortified, as I was not, and better reckon as they enter. But I see myself inscribing the original message, and so bearing the responsibility of confusion.

§

The wall contains all books, which means, all books, both existent and imagined.

In the first category will be found all books bound in human leather, for instance. These are in a surprisingly well-stuffed room devoted to the art of anthropodermic bibliopegy, which thrived in the nineteenth century. It includes the specially commissioned solo editions of Sir John Cheeke's *Hurt of Sedition: How Grievous it is to a Common Welth*, and Richard Braithwaite's *Arcadian Princess*, each of the flesh of Mary Bateman, and later reported lost. There is also a side chamber devoted to books falsely claimed for anthropodermic bibliopegy, more likely to be encased in highly burnished goat or suchlike.

In the second category, that of books imagined, the entire Library of St. Victor can be held, even if Pantagruel himself did not hold it.

The Library of St. Victor is only known to Pantagruel by its catalogue. This the giant finds in Paris, *after he had stayed there a pretty space, and studied very well in all the seven liberal arts, it was a good town to live in, but not to die; for that the grave-digging rogues of St. Innocent used in frosty nights to warm their bums with dead men's bones.*

I myself have spent some time reading such titles as *The Duster or Foxtail-flap of Preachers, composed by Turlupin*—a work of diligent, single-minded, and necessary heresy, as described on the rear—

The Spectacles of Pilgrims bound for Rome—another singularity, a testimony to human short-sightedness, its cover reads—

and *The Practice of Iniquity, by Cleuraunes Sadden*—unsurprisingly lengthy, all of it Rabelaisian in its excess.

I have held the original Thomas Browne, his *Hydriotaphia* first published in 1658, and have felt its weight and breathed in its ancient smell just as surely as I held almost every fabulised volume described in Browne's posthumous *Musaeum Clausum*, the sealed museum, or the *Bibliotheca Abscondita* as it is otherwise known.

Another catalogue, effectively, containing imaginary objects alongside books. None of the fictive objects described by Browne are here in the wall—there are no objects at all, merely books. Nothing exists in this space aside from those books, not a candlestick holder, nor a cup to drink from. All light suffuses from above, indirectly, and thirst and hunger follow about and gnaw at the belly, and eventually expire, until the only nourishment still known and remembered is literary, or bookish. A feast the weight of verbiage. It is fortunate that ancient books do occasionally smell like cured meat.

And so, I have not seen the *neat Crucifix made out of the cross Bone of a Frogs Head*, which Browne describes.

Nor have I come across the *Batracchomyomachia*, some kind of battle between frogs and mice *neatly described upon the Chizel Bone of a large Pike's Jaw*, or the skin of a snake *bred out of the Spinal Marrow of a Man*, or the *Quandros*, a stone of absolutely vile colouration extracted from the head of a vulture. And much as I would like to see it too, there is naturally, in the here of the wall, not the *complete Head and Body of Father Crispin*, nor even just a piece of his remains, the skin so well mummified, dried, and parched, Browne claims it can bear inscription.

ECCE ITERUM CRISPINUS—behold Crispinus again, reads what is etched into Father Crispin's carapace. His preservation is no mark of distinction but owes to the happenstance of vault atmospherics.

The books if not the objects of Browne's entirely fabulised *Musaeum Clausum* are all present in the wall, however, and I myself have held the very poem listed, *found wrapt up in Wax at Sabaria, on the Frontiers of Hungary.*

So too have I fingered *an exact account of the Life and Death of Avicenna,* discovered at a vault in Montpellier, *when the Walls of that City were demolished by Lewis the Thirteenth.*

And some manuscripts *scattered by the Souldiers of the Duke of Bourbon,* and subsequently gathered, one must assume, though Browne does not say so.

And a book once *left in the hands of a Jew of Ragusa.*

In addition, some pieces stolen from a certain Julius Scaliger, then sold to the *Bishop of Mende in Languedock, and afterward taken away and sold in the Civil Wars under the Duke of Rohan.*

And an obscure tome, its covers clotted with damp, describing the *several Vegetables found on the Rocks, Hills, Valleys, Meadows at the bottom of the Sea.*

And last, a book which is not completely original—as perhaps none of Browne's entirely are—for it contains a passage resembling one by Polybius as rendered by Strabo, *that all the*

Strabo's book is extant outside the wall, unlike Browne's fabulations which materialise only within the here of the wall. I knew it formerly, and its description of Thule, or the region thereabouts.

—here there is no more land nor sea to look at, nor air to breathe, but a comingling of each, redolent of sea lungs, and being so described, this region of all things that are not things, this indeterminacy, is just as sure to declare without so much as saying A REDUCTION TO COMINGLING NOTHING for any creature there venturing—

I learned of Strabo, or something of Strabo, just as I came to know many other books by casual reading in my home city, and not by the strained reception to which the books of the wall are received.

And so it was, I already knew how the elements in the realm or vicinity of Thule are suspended, or in a suspended state, forming a substance upon which one cannot walk, or sail through, the substance resembling a large species of jellyfish known once to Mediterranean peoples. This comingling of air with mineral with soil and water would surely present a challenge to the organism of its discoverer, given how the discoverer's body parts will have been made of similar materials prone in a similar way to jellification. Logic then presumes that the discoverer, the man named Pytheas—as related by Polybius via Strabo—did not see the gelatinous realm at all, or only glimpsed it from a very safe distance where elements were not yet suspended in their relation to each other. His toe was still attached to his foot and was distinct from the floor of the vessel in which Pytheas travelled with a crew, for surely there were companions, although the persons of that ship are not recorded, and were sent thereby and by that not recording to their own comingling nothing.

§

The Greek imaginary must needs be expunged for which the Greeks themselves may be recruited. Not least of all Herodotus, father of history and father of lies—and barbarian-lover, added Plutarch. Herodotus set his own reckoning above the work of the Gods and against all fables and marvels, Greek or barbarian, that is to say, against all which is presumed physically impossible or is considered unnatural, or against nature. He rooted the faculty of understanding in men who have settled for their lot, *who have started to come to terms with their smallness,* even if this results in delusions of greatness, and so he placed it, the faculty of understanding, in those that have reached the threshold of the civilized—Persians, Egyptians, even the Scythian nomad. Each has begun to evacuate the world of its shadow forms and spectral edges. Stone memorials and stories of conquest are their first words, or gatherings of fact against oblivion, addressed to a cosmos that cares nothing for them and so cannot be said to care or not care or even be indifferent in the matter of any of this here described. Here we are, and we are a people, they essentially say, and we are worthy of the historian's pen. Our existence must be recorded and will be known, not as a song, but as a chronicle of events. This turn to fact would turn out to be the most fatal of all turns—placing man at the centre of inspection, the inspected inspector, raising man as the final myth, the first and last fabricant—bewildered, at last, in the exercise of reason.

§

Being a cautious traveller, I did not enter the wall at once but attempted to know of it better first. With there being no trees in this landscape about it, nor vegetation of the woody sort besides the low scrub that brushed my ankles at intervals for weeks before my arrival, I could not construct an inspecting platform but walked back from the wall, and then away to the left and to the right to see from all groundward angles. No angle gave anything different to the one took before, or the one took after. Leftward gave nothing up that rightward had not shown. The wall is continuous for some days walk each way one will presume, and its curvature can scarcely be registered by looking down and along. The wall does not diminish to a point either, as an endless wall might, but this may be due to my failing sight as it might be the consequence of a line that has gradually curved its way out of vision. Of its composition little can be said. The wall is rendered with lime making the workmanship—the hefting and decision that can be seen in an edifice of irregular blockwork—impossible to see, and so to decipher. Little can be read from the lime render itself, the strokes of the pallet have gone and were difficult in any case as meaningful traces of work and labour, indecision and return, since the object of rendering is to conceal the motions of construction, whereas blockwork prominently displays it and in the case of the Inca boasts impossible joints, their needless labour of carving angles

45

and the imprints of angles in other stones that imprint in other stones and so on, and which suggest a kind of boastfulness, or a calm and knowing pride, a profligate expenditure of energies in any case which this wall in lime could not match, nor need it, having no call to boast otherwise and over the greater pride of its considerable length. As is typical with lime renders, the exterior does not fail in patches and detach, for the wall breathes slowly by its pores. It has weathered gradually and uniformly leaving a diminishing floor of dust extending outward several paces at the base. The material is so light that each footfall and rise very nearly erases its own print by the breeze of the walking foot, and it creaks, the dust, and is soon cast over with fresh dust by the gentle winds of the region. But to return to the wall by the door, this segment was nothing except the region of the doorway. With the extent of the wall reckoned, the doorway may be figured as reduced in its solitariness to a pinpoint, a punctum, but also magnified in its very singularity as the only feature upon a long surface, the only blemish in the continuity of its breadth, a blemish that was also a defining mark. Due to the architectural specifics—the fact of it being only wall and then singular door—there was no divining of the wall further by these means. Reluctant nonetheless to venture within without exerting the powers of human inspection to their fullest, I resolved to lift myself into the air.

§

A platform of the sort that could end a siege is what I saw in my mind's eye but would never build for the lack, actually the complete absence of wood. It was the kind of structure necessary to gain vantage of the wall and spy the interior, or at least gain perspective on the wall itself and measure its inward extent. In different circumstances, the people of the region would be induced by words if they were of the same lip, or by actions if they were not, and amass and contrive a structure for me to stand atop of. We would establish its base and give the thing round solid blocks of timber to roll on, and upon these raise it and build it, the raising and the building relying on the structure itself, around which we would duck in and out, and crawl and grasp at the beams, the all of it narrowing but robustly to the heights, and these might sway a little too in the wind or from the percussion of those climbing below and from the wheels that would shift against their wedges. Only there were no people living in this region before the wall, and those I met with last could not be induced by words or by actions to travel with me. When I spoke to them, my words left heavy in the craw.

The last people to be seen before the flat expanses before the wall were customed to turn over their infants to the slopes of the last hill, laid in lines, tethered to rocks on its coldest side, not to die from exposure but for the healing of their various ailments, much as midwives and doctors in a subsequent century would place ill and ailing new-borns in a permanently cooled casket—total body cooling, they called it, a restorative hypothermia. The contraption sucked warmth away and turned it out. Against all sense and instinct this cold chamber did work to cure them and allow those cured to live long enough to become sick with something else. The top and sides were made of glass, or something glass-resembling, through which they would watch it happen.

The oddness of the door must be measured against the habit of having a gatehouse. Here there were none. The greater walls of this world are usually studded by the structures, allowing guards to be kept, and for the preparation of hot tar and falling objects along the admitted territory, the floor often lined with traffic-beaten stone but also some of the external filth of the land trod inwards—if not too some inner filth trod outwards—a space, neither entirely inside, nor fully outside, fit for the activity of welcoming or expunging, a corridor, an in-between, that the gatehouse arches over and seeks to dominate entirely, hence its typicality. The gateway is the weakest point, and so attention is usually lavished there, and with it the gatehouse rises a good distance above all else in its vicinity. It was irregular to see the wall not break step to signify and counter-act that weakness—the admission of a doorway—with a demonstration of further height and ornament and battlement. The top of the wall was itself entirely flat, the limewash lapping over at a curve. Knowing the barest specifics of this wall before entry was not possible without gaining altitude, and of gaining altitude there was no possibility. I did not think of building a tower or any other contraption—to do so would be an indulgence of the mind—but settled to not knowing until the moment itself. Wasting no further effort outside, I would travel inside. The flat before the greater wall supplied nothing of its own that could be built with, and the nearest hill, where infants lay, was too distant to afford any kind of vantage over it. I had stood there surrounded by their desolate voices and had seen nothing. In a few hundred years or perhaps just a century or two infants would be subjected to something similar, I read, but sanctioned by science, and more closely monitored too, which is how that age found security.

The balloon was sewn of a patchwork and filled with heated air from the bones of the smaller creatures that roamed and died and left their little skeletons to dry against the sun of the flat. It was much as Pantagruel feared from the grave-digging rogues of St. Innocent, only the nights were not frosty, there were no rogues, and the bones were not of men but vermin. The balloon itself did leak gas and complain with it, and seemed to mimic those sounds which carry from the intestine to the surface of the belly.

Each valley was ordinary in its shaping when viewed from the perspective of its beginning. The ridge along which I strode left the plains where peoples were tied to the soil for the upper mountains where nomads wandered the slopes. Over these I would pass for the long descent to the flat and the wall.

The valleys were met before the mountain. The mountain was overcome before the flat, and the flat was transected before the wall. These valleys were numerous in their occasioning from the ridge. Another valley, and yet another, each with its own eroding, valley-forming river letting out below the scree. These rivers were not evident in their fount and were seen only as silver trails when the sun touched their lower ways. The dry slope accumulated by the ridge served as the initial sign of the basin before the fount, or spring, emerged and caused it to trickle. All circumstantial details.

§

A non-prolific ridge-side scree could hardly be distinguished from one which would be, properly speaking, valley-spawning. Looking outward from the ridge, and by approximating, squinting, and divining, only the sight of the distant basin could identify a valley-forming scree from one which would not proliferate. Which meant no valley could be viewed from its origins alone and all origins were suppositions besides.

§

The river grew from its loose rocks and little cuts and then minor and major tributaries, and nourished each basin as it widened, frothed, then amassed and boiled and finally let itself into the indeterminate realm of subterranean caves and flows that was each valley terminus. This was the fate of every valley here created—and that, properly speaking, was the anomaly of every formation—bounded by the upper scree, and, far below, and at its widest extent, by the high buttressed rock into where all water seeped and below which all things that floated or might roll on the riverbed were taken. There was some travel upward too from the subterranean realm, and fishes did appear in the lower reaches of the broadest point of the valley, but these soon perished, being unused to the light, and so the valley dwellers hardly fished, and there was no tradition of fishing among them.

—in *The Metaphor of Fish*, a rare and understudied early nineteenth century report on culture, and which includes, somewhat inexplicably, numerous etchings of extinct subspecies, it is argued that all cultures with a few notable exceptions incorporate metaphors of fish and fishing in their imaginaries, prime among them is the fateful belief in reaching out, or forward, into or across some unknown, and the accompanying paradox of a void that replenishes even as it swallows. Against which it is suggested of landlocked cultures that they exist in relation to the sky, their equivalent deep, but have no analogous conception of casting upward and hauling back riches, or of falling upward neither—

Each valley is marked off by a monument on the ridge, with the walkway so narrow at times a sign must be straddled if it is to be passed. Simple in their construction, often a mere rock raised and monumentalised by its upending. On every stone an inscription proclaiming the idea lived below—to which all swear fealty or are formed in fealty to—and which orients each society in every respect, including the thinking life of every inhabitant.

§

In the order of the idea, thought is oriented to its absolute. On most memorials the conclusion too is later inscribed, declaring the outcome of living by that singular conception.

The first ideas met with on the ridge are the simplest, and these monuments bear such words as Beauty, or Truth— those are the early words and valleys as I remember them.

The accompanying outcome is also recorded in these initial cases, indicating that the life of those valleys is concluded, with a few words most often sufficing to summarise what life according to a single idea will mean. RENDERED HISTORICAL is most commonly favoured as the recorded outcome, but frequently also OBLITERATED, or ANNULLED, if only to vary the work of monumentalising past life, or occasionally, and to vary this work still more, the lengthier, OBLIVION REIGNS AGAIN, or some such like expression.

Somehow, and this is somewhat extraordinary, every phrase used to encapsulate the death of a civilization carries with it a tinge of melodrama that cannot be expunged.

The inscription is at times more detailed—the sheer face of each monument permitting—and so it is recorded on one valley tombstone that its inhabitants, who were living according to the idea of ABSOLUTE MIGRATION, contrived to rise up the valley rim.

§

The rim becomes so steep that climbing upwards is defeated by the fall of scree coming downwards, and so they dug, or burrowed horizontally at the highest point they could reach before their defeat. A large number worked at the driving in of wedges and picks. They were sustained by the agricultural work of those below and the childrearing to replace generations of excavators who got hurt by the splinters of rock they hewed at, frequently struck by shards about the body and the eyes. The accidents had been occurring for decades, but even then they still occurred *more often than might have been expected,* as Herodotus writes of a different matter.

§

OF A DIFFERENT MATTER. Debilitating splinters were once suffered long before by a people wishing to isolate themselves on their peninsular. These peninsular dwellers hoped to cut through their land on the mainland side so to let the sea encompass and thereby fortify their position. Once again those working at the rock were injured *more often than might have been expected* by shards of stone, and mostly in the eye—this being odd given their custom of squinting tightly, and with precision timing, when striking down. Asking the Priestess at Delphi what was hindering their work by rendering them so very prone to accident and injury, they were given the following answer—*Zeus would have made an island, had he willed it.* In oracular terms this was unusually blunt and straightforward, leaving others to suggest this detail is a perfect example of Herodotus simply *making things up.* Having received their reply, the Cnidians as they were known, stopped digging, and surrendered to the approach of their oppressors.

Which most of it made sense to this valley too, and the Delphic line could be applied very nearly word for word, adjusted simply by exchanging *passage* for *island.* And thusly it is recorded on the monument. And that they all perished too.

Prevented against outward migration they would eventually flee from everything that issued inside their own minds, migrating from all customs and ties and relations, driven of an unquenchable restlessness that turned on their selves, a self-divulgement that had all the features of surface mining— it left them torn open. This was the fate of those oriented by ABSOLUTE MIGRATION within a bounded context. It has to be the least destructive example of that tendency to migrate to all corners, claiming each, but then shrinking as all empires eventually do before the impossibility of absolute possession.

§

Not all valleys are rendered complete and consigned their history, in which case the inscription is left pending. And yet, in one such valley the end of its living, and the beginning of its history, might just as well have been claimed. Its inhabitants barely lived enough to sustain their existence. This I glimpsed from curiosity, by leaving the high ridge for its own steep circumferences, and from which I saw how its people generally lay about and lived a vegetive life, grazing on the small berries and plants they shuffled toward and ate more or less by impulse and reflex, procreating too in a similar manner and when their bodies happened to collide. The birth and subsistence of their infants, outmost in its neglect, was just about sufficient to maintain a small population that could grow no stronger than the plants and edible fungi found existing not above head height when the person who eats them is prostrate.

In another valley with no concluding inscription the reigning idea was that *nothing can be judged until it is ended*. The effects were largely similar to the valley I met with before, only its inhabitants were often also upright on their legs. In the situation of this idea, all judgements were made when they no longer applied, which meant that for the duration of any person, or thing, or activity, all evaluative terms were held in reserve. All persons existed without their ever receiving accolade or dismissal but were robustly evaluated in their personhood, minutely, at length, and for so long as memory served, once they had died. It was entirely fitting to speak ill of the dead, given it was not possible to speak ill of the living. Actions too proceeded without the application of any framework of value but were judged severely as soon as they were concluded. This presented a challenge to the non-judgement of living persons. In principle anyone involved in actions would be judged by implication as and when those actions concluded. Persons could carry judgements from one action to the next, accumulating judged actions about their person, and so accumulating conceptions of their own worth, of how they might be evaluated *in the round*. Here the valley dwellers faced two divergent options and so lived along two possible lines of flight. For some, actions were divorced entirely from persons, which meant personhood was lived as an actionless thing. For others, whole lives were enacted as a single gesture, and so persons were still considered capable of actions, even if each person was defined by a single, drawn-out movement. Either way, the effect was the same, a kind of non-living. The art of living without judgement was the art of continuity of form. And hence, some lived so slowly they hardly seemed to move. They progressed according to a severely delayed developmental gradualism, where a bodily act or remark of the arm was reduced to a kind of glacial perfection, or planetary inertia, that was serene as it was painful, the muscles coming to spasm and then near-solidify in their stasis.

It was much as Solon the Athenian advised the tyrant Croesus—as Herodotus relates—declaring that Croesus could not be judged to have been a happy man, least of all the happiest of men, until all his deeds were done, and Croesus was dead. *Often enough God gives a man a glimpse of happiness, and then utterly ruins him,* so Solon said, or so Herodotus reports. But Solon's teaching was extraordinarily limited in its application. It was applied only to the tyrant and the tyrant himself did not heed it. Whereas in the valley below the requirement to look to the end of everything brought about a more lasting transition. If no evaluative term had application whilst its object lived, and none could be judged by others, or deem themselves happy, or fortunate, or wise, or healthy, no person living could think themselves happy, nor could they be self-consciously happy, fortunate, wise, or healthy, or even experience happiness, or good fortune, or wisdom, or health, or at least know their experience ought to be one of happiness, good fortune, wisdom, or health. Which meant there was no conception of living in happiness within this vocabulary, nor of any other designated state of living goodness. Neither could they view any habit of living in negative terms, not until its victim or perpetrator was dead. And if positive terms, such as health, or vivacity, are generally associated with the living state, these concepts were not applicable in death, and so hardly existed as terminal judgements either. It was not possible to say, this or that person was once healthy if the term had no retroactive purchase. All conceivable evaluative ideas that might be applied to any individual or situation or thing, could no longer have a hold on the living, could not be consequential to them. Which meant all evaluative terms were summary judgements, and largely negative for that reason. Living was really only understood as a state of dying, seeing how it was only ever evaluated from the aspect of the dead and the idea of death itself was unmoored from any ceremonial attachment. Whilst the valley dwellers were able to evaluate the deeds and misdeeds of their ancestors, neighbours, and kin—albeit by negation, so long as they were confirmed dead and departed, and they had no way of interacting meaningfully with the living including their own living selves, this did not simply entail being unable to decide between good and bad actions or adjudicate between friends and enemies— indeed people had not the depth of behaviour that such terms might rely upon. It meant absolute paralysis in knowing whether a mouldy apple would be better to eat than a ripe one. The results were utterly debilitating and will scarcely be pictured, the inhabitants dealing with their immediate surrounds in a state of complete neutrality—another unapplicable word— some moving, most not, but all of them having no means of preferring one thing above another, and taking no investment at all in the activity of living, not even insofar as living might be understood as a kind of killing—killing moments, killing earlier versions of selves, which was why they took such pleasure—even if the word could not apply—in gathering around the dead. There were outbreaks of extraordinary violence—for after all, why not—but mostly calm dejection persisted, and anything resembling human community—a pact between the living— gave way before a kind of retreating judgementalism, directed only at the dead, the unavailable, the unalterable nothing.

Solon also related the story of two young men of Argos whose mother prayed in a fit of enthusiasm and pride to the goddess Hera that her sons, who were extraordinarily well endowed with physical strength and public adulation at that point, should be granted *the greatest blessing that can fall to mortal man.* And so it was, the two lads fell asleep *and that was the end of them, for they never woke again.* This was *heaven-sent proof of how much better it is to be dead than alive,* writes Herodotus.

Thracians express a similar sentiment. When a baby is born, the family sits round and mourns at the thought of all of the sufferings the infant must endure now it has entered the world. Although Herodotus does not put it in these terms, their extended lament might be viewed as a method of pain-investigation, or be seen as an early type of accountancy, a dormant economism. Thracian lament amounts to a tally against life, for the family goes through the whole catalogue of human sorrows and makes itself miserable as each and every type of human suffering known to them is described and given its place in their cabinet of earthly pain. But when somebody dies, Herodotus continues, the situation is its opposite, and they bury with merriment and rejoicing, and point out how happy the dead must now be, or if not happy, at least fortunate, and of how many further miseries they have escaped. The catalogue of human sorrow is again listed, only this catalogue is now a column of sorrows that cannot be endured, pains that will not be felt, because all feeling has left the body.

The contrasting tradition may be found among the Egyptians. When the rich among them hold a party, and once they have finished their meal, a man carries round for all to contemplate a wooden corpse—painted so as to look real, though diminutive in stature—and says, *Look upon this body as you drink and enjoy yourself, for you will be just like it when you are dead.* These were the same Egyptians who lived among the crocodile, or knew of those who did, a creature possessed with eyes like a pig's and fangs all out of proportion. Herodotus considers it the *only animal to have no tongue and a stationary lower jaw*, a description which produced many subsequent illustrations of this anatomical curiosity, each demonstrating in turn that the artist had never actually encountered such a creature. Similarly the Hippopotamus, once described as the nadir or Herodotean zoology, had a mane and tail and a voice like a horse. It carried a hide *so thick and tough that when dried it can be made into spear-shafts*. Last of all, the winged snake, which flies to Egypt from Arabia each spring, and comes to travel across a narrow mountain pass where the skeletons of their predecessors are found piled in heaps. These serpents are met at that place by the ibis which kills them as they pass over.

Not all ideas could be given their reality in a respective valley and be bred to excess—the purity of an idea realised to its end. Herodotus claims that when Persians meet in the streets, if they are of the same rank, *they do not speak but kiss—their equals on the mouth, those somewhat superior on the cheeks. A man of greatly inferior rank prostrates himself in profound reverence. After their own nation they hold their nearest neighbours most in honour, then the nearest but one—and so on, their respect decreasing as the distance grows, and the most remote being the most despised. Themselves they consider in every way superior to everyone else in the world, and allow other nations a share of good qualities decreasing according to distance, the furthest off being in their view the worst.* Thus, the Persian outlook, as Herodotus presents it, depends on exclusion by degrees, a logic of prejudice which applies to the telling of it too by Herodotus. This particular idea cannot be held, or told or enacted, without the presumed existence of an alienable other—outsiders who will be made to suffer if only in judgement. And so it was that no valley—sequestered, isolated, confined by its inalienable horizon—and no valley people, could be organised by this particular fancy or anything like it. That notion and its associates only had application on the plains below the ridge. Here cultures intermingled and came to understand themselves in relation to those they alienated, which generated a worldview, a set of conceits, and various fealties too, and a whole picture of the universe that was simply unavailable in its hubris, in its expansive self-aggrandisement, to those in the valleys that gave off from the ridge.

§

From the plains rose a long and growing ridge spawning minor watersheds, each wrapping round to enclose its valley as the letter J turns to enclose itself when placed alongside another, JJ, and then another, JJJ, to complete what was, effectively, a displaced ribcage.

ՐՐՐՐՐՐՐՐՐՐՐՐՐՐՐՐՐՐՐՐՐՐՐՐՐՐՐՐՐՐՐՐՐՐՐՐ
JJJJJJJJJJJJJJJJJJJJJJJJJJJJJJJJJJJJJJ

Within each enclosed space a people lived, every enclosure a different custom dealing in divergent ways with the same predicament—their absolute confinement. Nothing could achieve definition against an exterior something, or exceed itself in its direction, and so inner exclusions, or internal outsides were drawn and reached intensities rarely encountered on the plains. The exterior was placed inside its people in this way, and they defined themselves against it.

Every act of internal division and inner violence related by Herodotus had its respective valley, taking their inertias from when the West was still young and experimenting with its power. These valleys were so numerous a happenstance of this kind should come as no surprise. And so, the exact same mound of earth—or a mound measuring up to the same particulars—appears in one of these valleys just as Herodotus describes, that is to say, *the greatest work of human hands apart from the Egyptian and Babylonian.* It is the tomb of Alyattes, father of Croesus. The base is built of huge blocks, the rest a heap of dirt raised by the toil of the king's tradesmen, craftsmen, and prostitutes, on the top of which there still survived to the days of Herodotus five phallic pillars with inscriptions to show the amount of work each had done, with the king's prostitutes having by far the largest share. This did not honour their effort, but was a further sign, a demonstration, of the undiminished potency of the king.

Within the displaced ribcage of the valleys, women suffered all the fates that the West, still young, was working out. These violences would in some cases set a line to the universal, to the absolute merciless nothing within those communities, allowing men to form themselves in relation to their degradation, their abjection, and elevate themselves by way of it. Here too were enacted forms of bodily and psychic abuse that managed to simultaneously figure the feminine body as an object of worship, as something to, in a way, revere, mostly in relation to its external frame, and indirectly by attachment to the womb that was taken to symbolise the valley, their universe, the giver and creator, a lamentably divine, unimpeachable grace.

§

With the plains several days behind me, the land on which I trod rose and took upon itself atypical features pressed with the might of a creator's hand at either side to produce a long and running ridgeline bordered by extended, finger-like depressions that were its corresponding valleys, each in the shape of the letter U.

UUUUUUUUUUUUUUUU

∩∩∩∩∩∩∩∩∩∩∩∩∩∩∩∩

These valleys were distinguished from each other by languages that were entirely divorced and owed no common ancestor. Meeting at each valley terminus, those straying into the neighbouring valley had nothing much to say and returned home.

There could be no engagement, least of all an attempt to find out which people was the more venerable, and hence, no such enquiry of the sort related by Herodotus, wherein there was some debate over whose was the more ancient and perhaps original civilization, the Egyptian, or the Phrygian. The Egyptian pharaoh, Psammetichus, decided to resolve the matter by having two babies snatched from their homes, one of Phrygian issue, the other of Egyptian descent, and, thus taken, were sent to live with a shepherd under order never to speak a word in their company. The children were to stay in an isolated cottage with the shepherd bringing in goats from time to time to ensure the infants were not overly wanting for milk. It is likely they suckled directly when littlest, or perhaps the shepherd drew into a cup. The idea was to find out what would be their first meaningful utterance once the infants advanced beyond their insensate noise, from speech sounds consequent of the mouth, the tongue, and the gums. Which is to say, the idea was to find the first definite word which arrived after all the other, inchoate sounds they made, all of them having come forth without the driving, word-forming presence of the informed mind to organise and tame them. And so it was, two years later the shepherd opened the door to the cottage and was greeted by both children, *running up to him,* as Herodotus reports, *with hands outstretched* and pronouncing the word *becos.* This they repeated and they would not let off with saying it, and when the shepherd reported to Psammetichus, the pharaoh knew his experiment to be concluded, since *becos* is Phrygian for bread.

—they had seen the shepherd eating it when laid up themselves beneath a goat. Presumably the shepherd did not gesture at the orphans, and torment them, saying *becos, becos, becos,* since this would undermine the experiment and make senseless all of their suffering and neglect. It is possible the shepherd spoke in his sleep. But there were other versions of the story. The Greeks liked to think that Psammetichus had the babies brought up by women whose tongues he cut out. These women could not talk in their sleep, or resist the urge to sing to their children, or tell them fond things about their tummies, or their toes, or the roundness of their rumps. It makes sense that the dawn of reason is associated with the Greeks.

No such experiment could be done in the valleys described and due to the reasons presented, but the pharaoh's assumption of linguistic pre-eminence did seem extendable to them, with each valley people having grown from a fragment of the creator's fingernail, a fragment which contained the elements of life comingled with the rudiments of each respective linguistic system.

§

The Histories was the original bestiary. Each creature therein further stretches the claim that Herodotus was the true father of history. Or at least, historiography will only find its roots in Herodotus, and so in the Greek world, by admitting its development was at the cost of purging itself of speculative elements, residual mythologies, incursions against reason of nightmare and fancy. The only continuity to be found, beyond a pretence of even-handedness—Herodotus often considers more than one version of a story—is a preoccupation with the psychological life of actors long gone to oblivion. Herodotus intrudes on peoples whose outlooks are never recoverable. He makes claims on the perception of those whose subjecthoods were formed of the accumulated trouble of their experience, from untranslatable smells, and sights, and sensations, which the historian could not simulate. His characters are consequently flat, and their flatness is the form taken by truth as it returns to *The Histories* after all.

When the Arabians gather frankincense, they burn storax brought them from Greece by the Phoenicians. This to drive away the flying snakes, the same creatures which invade Egypt and lie piled where the ibis kills them as they pass over. Some have claimed the skeletal remains are so regularly stacked that the ibis must have a mathematical mind, or alternately, that the ibis has a preference for order, or at least, the ibis finds disorder unpleasant, or if not unpleasant, not particularly pleasing, so that in sum or by the elimination of present hypotheses, the ibis finds arrangement satisfying in the most banal and symptomatically human of ways, and sides with humanity against the brutes in that respect. Others have suggested the ibis actually has a mocking mind, and that its rigid organisation of snake ribs and snake vertebrae is a form of observational comedy, a performance piece in the furthest mountains where the ibis recreates the futility it perceives from the air of the organisational, brick and bone stacking habits of the civilized. These snakes, the Arabians say, would swarm and multiply but for the manner of their conception and birth. The female seizes the neck of the male during the release of sperm and chews at that point in the neck of the male with the dry, mauling determination their kind display—it is the anatomy of the jaw that defines the anatomy of will in the order of serpents—and she continues to hold, and tighten, until it is bitten through. The young avenge their father, Herodotus records, thereby extending to the animal realm one of the prime motives which propels the psychological drama of *The Histories*, gnawing at her insides until they eat their way out.

It is fortunate the flying snake is largely confined to Arabia, and that it does not breed and spread like birds or men, or the prolific hare, *in which superfetation occurs,* writes Herodotus. Cut one open, *and you will find in a hare's womb young in all stages of development, some with fur on, others with none, others just beginning to form, and others, again, barely conceived.* Not so the lion—the other extreme of the hair-coated mammals—where the lioness, Herodotus states, gives birth not simply to the cub, but expels her womb with it, her innards torn by the cub since it first began to stir and flex its claws, all but destroying its home before it was birthed with it.

Seeking to explain how Darius, son of Hystaspes, and king of Persia extracted his 360 talents of gold-dust from the Indians in tax, Herodotus tells how they fetch it from the desert and had a good amount stashed and ready for Darius to claim as his due. There is a kind of ant, a gold-digging ant, *bigger than a fox, though not so big as a dog,* living out in the wasteland. Or that is how Herodotus tells it and Megasthenes seems to agree. *They are not inferior in size to wild foxes,* writes Megasthenes more than a century on. The great voyager Nearchus, of the army of Alexander the Great, actually saw their skins, writes Strabo, and thought the largest of them to rival the size of a leopard. For his part, and centuries later still, Pliny the Elder has the gold-digging ant the size of *an Egyptian wolf* and the *colour of a cat.* The creature also has horns. There is a letter reputedly sent to Hadrian, or perhaps it was to Emperor Trajan, in which the ants are described as the size of puppies with claws like those of lobsters. In the third century after Christ, the ants are the size of *very big* dogs, according to the Latin compiler of curiosities, Gaius Julius Solinus, and have feet like a lion. These gold-digging monsters are not to be confused, as they often were, with the very different lion-resembling ant, otherwise known as the ant lion. It will be found in the notorious *Physiologus,* an early Christian text containing various fanciful creatures, each monstrously didactic in form and presentation. The ant lion of that book has the head of a lion and the body of an ant. The head eats meat which the body, being vegetarian, cannot digest, and so the chimeric beast eventually dies. A lesson against things of a dual nature, or of a double mind, by one reading.

In the late seventh century catalogue of marvellous creatures known as the *Liber Monstrorum*, gold-digging ants are now black and have six legs. By the eleventh century, Anglo-Saxon authors specify them as big as dogs—the breed is not mentioned—and with *feet like grasshoppers*. They are, moreover, *of red and black colour*, which fits perfectly with Pliny the Elder, who never specified which breed of cat he had in mind.

The Persian king had a few of them held captive, writes Herodotus, and would probably know better than any their exact dimension. To others it would be a question of visiting the palace and asking which deep pit to look down about the palace grounds. It was necessary to do the subsequent looking by daylight, not because the pits could not be lit by a suspended lantern, actually lanterns would be just as necessary during the day, but for the simple reason that the king made a point of never roping off a hole and declared, in so diligently not doing, that his menagerie was always open to chance arrivals. The onlooker might yet wonder if the captive ants were representative of their breed, and whether they had grown in captivity, fatted by inactivity, or become shrunken for the lack of good digging. These onlookers presumed the Persian king to be as miserly with his gold in regard of the ants as he was with anyone else, and so the king would give them just as little, which is to say none of it, as he gave anyone who was not stranded in a pit and was hungry for it. But if the ants could not be fatted by gold, this did not preclude one another, nor did it rule out chance arrivals—assuming the ants were omnivorous. But then again, perhaps these ants, the king's ants, were only caught because they were abnormally small, or weak, or grossly large and slow and slothful. The onlooker, or down-looker, might also ask if the pit itself, which is to say the pit aspect, changes the aspect of the ant from the position of the viewer, with the same ant pursuing one's camel across a desert looking somewhat different.

The question of size aside, this ant burrows underground and throws sand up in heaps just as Greek ants do with earth, only the desert ants are so much bigger that the mounds they create will be proportionally greater. The sand for which they have a taste is rich in gold, which is why they mound it over, and this is what the Indians go for, each man with three camels abreast, writes Herodotus. He will always ride a female of the species, and of these only a female *who has as recently as possible dropped her young*. This creature thus encumbered travels with two sacrificial males flanking either side on a leading rein. Since the Greeks are familiar with what the camel looks like, Herodotus mentions only two specifics which may be novelties, first, that the camel *in its hind legs has four thighs and four knees*, second, *its genitals point backwards towards its tail*—Herodotus is right about the backward-pointing genitals, wrong about the legs.

The object is to reach the mounds of sand during the hottest part of the day when the ants retreat underground. Though habituated to the climate, the ant is not fully adjusted to it, and cannot bear the heat despite its armour. Actually, this armour might be responsible for it not bearing the heat—naturalists have always had such roundabout ways of talking—some have said that the carapace does hiss as it gathers the heat and boils the innards, and so the ants will not take it long before bubbling from the inside out. Few allow themselves to be caught in the sun, and those that do will be swiftly dried through, and disconnected, as the sinews crack under the pressure of the light, the head from the thorax, this thorax from the abdomen, these parts rolling along during high winds if they are not soon filled with sand and then buried. The leg armour, hollowed out in a similar way, can be worn about the shins or lower arm. Those who make for the mounds prepare for the heat by soaking themselves with the last of the water. This gives their outline a haze. Reaching the place where the gold is piled and mingled with sand they fill their bags and make retreat as fast as they can, for the heat soon subsides and the ants emerge, and *smell them,* writes Herodotus, *and at once give chase; nothing in the world can touch these ants for speed,* tells he, *so not one of the Indians would get home alive, if they did not make sure of a good start while the ants were mustering their forces.* The male camels either side soon drag—they are slower in general, reluctant too at the leading rein—and fall away when cut loose, one at a time as is best done, and are presumably collapsed at the ankles, crawled over, and killed by their pursuers to the advantage of those still in flight. The females are kept going *by the memory of their young,* and this gets them home. The journey is costly in camels yet so profitable in gold that the expenditure of the male of the species can be justified.

In the account of Megasthenes, given in his *Indica*—a book lost and then recovered as fragments from those who quoted it—the ants are likened to moles and have extensive mines underground. They run with incredible speed and *live by the produce of the chase.* The robbery of the ants is managed by leaving the flesh of wild animals at various places to divert the ants and disperse them too—a single ant is dangerous; a swarm is impossible. The plain itself is covered by their hillocks, piled in regular order, and would be effulgent in the joy those heaps could radiate to all onlookers but for the insects. The dust, once stolen, is laid on wagons, torn at by the swiftest horses, those driving them taking care to shield their eyes—many have been struck down by the combined brightness of the sun above and the shineful piles below. Several wagons will not return, their crew having fought and lost to the ants. But with the profits to be gained, the loss of companions is considered endurable by the survivors.

About the motives of the giant ants themselves little is said, with suppositions varying from their lusting after gold—a drive resembling that of the camel riders and horse-drivers allowing each ant to feel robbed—to the other most commonly adduced motive, their working under the constraints of their instinct, as the smaller ants do. Surely something so small, or at least basic, so crisp and dry as insectile life, cannot deliberate or covet. Mounds are mere leftovers of excavation; pursuit and killing is simply good border keeping.

The ant, here now and hereafter the *humble* ant, was usually taken as a model of Christian virtue in the medieval bestiaries, duty-bound, industrious, self-denying, and co-operative in their submission to ant-life. And so it was opposed to the weasel, for instance, which conceives through the mouth and gives birth from the ear, or perhaps it was the other way round. Either way, the weasel, as it sits in groups, preoccupied entirely with engorging and extruding, has little passage remaining for taking in the word of God, nor available attention for doing much good with it, or doing anything else beyond its most immediate business, which is all in the head.

§

§

Alongside its books, the wall seemingly contained all objects, or certainly those written down, including a Crucifix made of a very small bone, possibly from a lizard; the jaw of a fish on which an extraordinary detail is carved from the lower regions of the forest floor where frogs and mice are commonplace; a snake skin that smells of bone marrow; a stone so putrid in its colouration it caused me to retch at the sight of it; and a mummified corpse the skin of which was so hardened by treatment it is carved as wood is carved and bears the words

Ecce iterum Crispinus, or take another look at old Crispinus—he will not rise without cracking.

Mostly rooms are devoted to singular objects, such as the one containing codpieces, and another chastity belts. In one chamber I found every known and unknown icon in which St. Nicholas fasts from the nipple—the aboriginal refuser. And within a side-chamber various statuettes misattributed to this legend. These may or may not depict the Woman of the Apocalypse. There is also a chamber that contains every single lump of myrrh ever inscribed in a book, or roll, or tablet, and another in which each speck of dust ever mentioned, when written of in the form of *a speck*, that is, rather than as motes, or as a layer, there is another room for them.

Nicholas was of such precocity when it came to fasting, so it goes, he only drank from the nipple on Wednesdays and Fridays. Or he only drank *once* from the nipple on those days. Some accounts are very specific on that detail. *Nicholas took but one sip from the nipple on Wednesdays and Fridays*, it is written. This might have been a very long sip, as some infants are indeed known to sup. It also left Saturday to Tuesday, and Thursday too, for engorgement. So much for St. Nicholas.

§

On the treeless steppe north of the Black Sea live the Scythian nomads who keep no record of their past but know themselves to be the youngest of all nations, as Herodotus relates, and, when presented with the anus of a mare, *insert a tube made of bone and shaped like a flute*, says he, *and blow.*

—the objective is *to inflate the mare's veins with air and so cause the udder to be forced down* and be made available for milking—

Their kingdom is limited at its northernmost reaches *because of falling feathers,* by one account. These feathers make it impossible to travel any further or even see what lies in the horizon.

§

§

The Scythians are entirely without qualities and deserve no respect having no accomplishments bar one, the single thing they have managed *better than anyone else on the face of the earth: I mean their own preservation,* writes Herodotus. In writing that, Herodotus demonstrates the underlying humanity of his outlook, for a lesser author would consider this achievement of a race without qualities to be its final indictment, and would say, *having no accomplishments, and deserving no respect, the Scythians have laid one last crime upon their world, the fact of their own preservation.*

But this decision to give record of those who minister to no other law than their own, may also be at the root of Herodotus' inhumanity, and the violence of all the rulers, and war parties, and impalers, women stranglers, child killers, and enslavers, whom Herodotus is at pains to preserve, *in all their accomplishment* and for posterity within *The Histories.* Often enough Herodotus will keep nameless those who do not deserve to be recorded. These do sometimes warrant oblivion in their disgrace, but more often than not in their lack of commitment to making their mark, to opening a wound for others to marvel at as it suppurates and crusts over. This strike against remembrance, the historian's oubliette, is never aimed for those who serve the foremost principle that the historian of peoples also works under, *each his own self-preservation,* which means the ability to resist invaders if not turn them into slaves or corpses, and do so for long enough to leave a trace, a set of artefacts, or at the very least the rumour of an existence for the historian to gather up. That resistance against destruction which relies upon the destruction of others, or if it does not, which resists oblivion by exemplary dying, is the condition of possibility for the historian's work, and so it is appreciated. It is a truism that all historians rely, whatever their intentions, upon the endurance of scars.

A secondary merit of the Scythians might be the manner of their flesh boiling in a landscape with little or no wood to boil with. As soon as the animal, let's say an ox, is strangled, the beast is skinned, de-boned, and the flesh packed inside the paunch and placed above the bone fire. *In this way an ox, or any other sacrificial beast, is ingeniously made to boil itself.*

§

As my shadow crossed the plains and entered the vicinity of the ridge, I did begin to look out for all the many things that could be remembered of Herodotus. By the time I reached the first rise, and my shadow shortened against the declivity, I expected to find the historian already there surveying the very same goods.

BUT THERE WERE no gifts of earth and water | no goat-footed race or men who sleep for six months in the year | no river so devoid of turbid water as the Borysthenes | no great pile of brushwood raised each year by a hundred and fifty wagon-loads of sticks | no sacrifice of prisoners of war in which rite their hands are cut off and thrown in the air and all of them left where they drop | no cloaks formed of scalps sewn together and made to look like the ones peasants wear | no quivers made of the skins of the right arm of the enemy, fingernails included | no skulls turned into drinking vessels, passed round by the host who tells the story of how each cup was once a relative who rose up against them | no women-men twisting the bark of the lime tree round their fingers as they prophesy | no mode of execution in which peccant soothsayers are gagged and bound and placed in a cart filled with sticks set alight and hauled by oxen that escape burning only if the pole of the cart is burnt through before they add their own fat to the conflagration | no bodies of kings coated with wax, their bellies slit, cleaned out, filled with aromatics, and sewn back up again | no entourage of enforced mourning with circular incisions made in the upper arm, heads shaved, and arrows thrust through their left hands | no burial of the butler and cook alongside the concubines with all of them strangled | no sacrificial servants stuffed with chaff | no dead horses mounted on broken wheels, a stout pole passed lengthways though each from tail to neck and the legs left dangling | no region where the earth is exclusively black | no dead men with poles driven through the neck and mounted on the dead horses which they seemingly ride, with each horse bitted and bridled | no freshly dead corpses laid on a cart and made to visit their friends | nobody who could be described as the best-looking man of his day | no eunuchs | no marriages that came to nothing | no men who should have become king but did not | no shrines | no vapour baths with hemp seeds thrown on hot rocks inside a tent that is crept into and enjoyed so much its occupant howls with pleasure | no griffins | no perfect rejection of foreign ways | no easterly winds | nobody shooting anyone else dead with a bow in a forest | no densely wooded hills | no consecrated ground | no claims to sensible conversation | no houses on stilts above water with hidden trapdoors and babies tied by the leg to stop them falling in | no horses fed exclusively on a diet of fish | no killing of men with women's brooches and subsequent change of fashion to a brooch-less tunic | no young men who claim ignorance of the harsh ways of the world | no king possessed by the spirit of Dionysus in the grip of the Bacchic frenzy subsequently murdered by his subjects for the disgrace of it | no cattle grazing backwards because their oddly shaped horns are impaled when grazing forwards | no salt spring which emerges tepid during the day and boils at night | no census bowl made of arrowheads, one arrowhead to a man, four inches thick and measuring 5000 gallons in capacity | no troglodytes swift of foot | no footprint left by Heracles admired for being three feet long | no Pillars of Heracles | no captain placed in irons with his head stuck through an oar-port | no river that will cure men and horses of the scab | no claim the country beyond the Danube is infested by bees | no locusts caught, dried, ground up, and drunk with milk | no race that thinks itself immortal and sends messages to the gods by killing its menfolk, these men thrown aloft and made to land on three javelins after hearing the words they must travel with | no mark of low birth | no race that does without names | no cursing the sun for wasting and burning the land | no people said never to dream | no drinking from another's hand or licking dust from it when there is no liquid | no secret messages tattooed to the scalp of a slave | no flaying a man's flesh in strips to make the chair of a judge | no sprinkling goat's urine on a child | no curing children of catarrh by burning the veins on their heads | no attempts to verify progeny by spectating as a child is born | no houses built of salt blocks | no efforts to throw off the Persian yoke | no Persian yoke | no need to endure being ruled by another man | no need to endure being ruled by a man | no tribe that could be described as more manly or law-abiding than any other | no organised community that has no concept of law or justice | nobody stoned to death | no contest between girls equipped with stones and a good throwing arm | no single arrow shot into the clouds to deny existence to the lord of lightening | no such thing as a trireme | no peoples known only for their diet of lice | no wives used in common | no wife related by blood | no blood relations | no betrothals | no accusations of fornication | no need to decide which party is telling the truth | no organised revolt or entity to revolt against | no lakes or ponds | no Hellespont | no forest containing all types of tree | no creature with a square face | no testicles good for curing diseases of the womb | no headless men with eyes in their chests | no marauders | no hoplites | no young men | no men embarking from ships | no declarations of war on the south wind | no marching in the desert | no burials in a sandstorm | no furthest point | no automatic killing of shipwrecked Greeks | no Black Sea | no coastline | no Amazons | no attempt to breed with the Amazons | no children born of the Amazons | no attempts to describe other peoples such as the Amazons | no anger of the gods | no artifices of man | no historians | no proto historians | no children born of the Greeks | no Greeks.

§

Free of Herodotus my feet trod the last of the shoulder to the first of the mountains where the ridge entered at the midriff. Used to path taking, I am habituated to the assumption that all paths, no matter their type or historical origin, are trod to some kind of sense and this sense will be found either by following a path, or by understanding the path in terms of its vacated historical context. These mountains tested that assumption.

The route then taken, such as it was, took along a path that had been trod down and set in place, but which struck me as confused, for it forked or splayed about, the major route never distinguishable from its tributaries, or at least routes exchanged priority. Some path lines re-joined after circuitous detours, others reached round a rise never to re-associate, and if they approached a neighbouring track, turned back as if by repulsion. This was my only evidence of the nomads who, if they were nearby, retreated just before I appeared.

§

IN THE REGION OF MOVABLE ROCKS, the fall of the foot finds insecurity with every step. These replies become suspicions, a natural conspiracy, one may think, already at work in the minor stones. Their mutual prompts had all the exuberance of cannon shot. Extended nudgings played at the larger ones still small enough for the foot to disturb, and from there to the embedded lumps wedged into the ground, susceptible even despite their part burial to the inertias of movement. These half-buried rocks would otherwise be relied upon, as walkers know who look for them and single them out for treading. Stood paused from the walking, worried at the movement and looking thereabout, it becomes apparent that to a stationary person nothing appears to move unless the eyes blink whereupon some shifting occurs, and this no parallax error.

—if Herodotus were still here to give them flesh, the Arimaspi or one-eyed folk would confirm it.

§

With Herodotus behind me I encountered the nomads. There was no unseeing them. These people were turned out of themselves as I presented myself to understand their outlook and travelled with it across the mountain chain and eventually through the highest pass.

The nomad, said I, makes a promise with each step and registers it fulfilled within each footfall. The foot rises and then falls elsewhere, measuring the duration of the promise and its extinction. This foot, I decided, does not define a lasting territory from which the promise extends, and so can have no orbit or home, or right of judgement where the reckoning is done. The nomadic promise might be judged to have been made in bad faith from the territory and perspective of another, or be taken as a sign of impotence, or at least of negligence. But here, or there where I came to walk, I came to see something not unlike what these words have in mind. All judgements must be misplaced if they last longer than a footfall.

I put this to the nomads themselves when they came near, and receiving no reply, but noticing how speech would not interrupt them, decided that the nomadic promise is kept within its realm of decision. As the nomad formulates each step, a step which is also a promise, that step, and that promise, establishes the very limit of the gesture. The nomad settles all scores as soon as they are made, meets all interests in the moment of their arousal. This seems to explain their silence against which the fall of my own feet sounds clumsily, and my words carry outward only on the condition they are fore-weighted. It seemed to me that my culture, before theirs, suffered a kind of halitosis. Its words reek of decay.

The rot is always down there—this is how the civilized see it—which is how Leonard Steaner was fined *for allowing his scabbed horse on the common.* Or William Marshall in 1668 for *casting his dunghill on the high road to the nuisance of passers-by,* or Thomas Illingworth *for allowing his swine to go in the churchyard,* or William Shaw for *making his jakes in the beck to the great nuisance of his neighbours.*

§

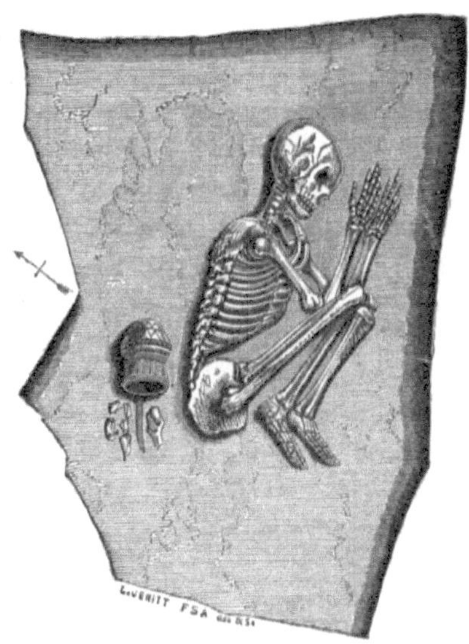

Rock Grave, Smerrill Moor.

§

Breathing out against his peer, this man in the hollow said the only hole Bateman needed to have dug was his own, and that his *Ten Years' Diggings in Celtic and Saxon Grave Hills* was a miss-spent and wasted decade, and Bateman hardly dug anyway, or only picked about the edges, having his men do the bulk of the work for him, and that this barrow by the hollow in which the man of the hollow lay half-buried, was one of those barrows Bateman picked over when he should have been preparing his own. Bateman's way was to dig a trench straight through the middle, in most cases, and then throw back the dug matter into the trench once finished, together with a little brass tag on which was embossed *Thomas Bateman* so that subsequent diggers would know why it was all up-side-down, or topsy-turvy, and why there were no bones or other grave goods left to marvel at. Occasionally the tag would be misspelt, as subsequent digs did confirm, suggesting that Bateman was either careless of his own good name, or employed careless assistants, which seems more likely. Most weeks Bateman averaged four barrows and on some days reached six or seven exhumed, and besides had barrows dug in other counties too by his fellow diggers, a Mr. Samuel Carrington of Wetton, who dug the barrows of Staffordshire, and a Mr. James Ruddock of Pickering, who did many of the mounds of Yorkshire. Ruddock was the less reliable of the two and would record in his notes, *dug a barrow near Pickering,* or *found these items in the dig I did after the one just mentioned near Pickering,* or such like, and did not think it needful to be any more specific. Bateman received news that Mr. James Ruddock of Pickering had died just as Bateman was completing the text of *Ten Years' Diggings.* This gave prompt for a footnote about how Mr. James Ruddock was *singularly imbued* with his passion for digging up mounds, even during his final illness, and that his passion would be as strong in death as it was in life. And so it was, in that Mr. James Ruddock did not even when he lived do much of the labour of digging up mounds himself. It would not be much different when he died, the work of digging then having one last assignment, one last consequence of his so-called passion—or the fact of his living and dying—when Ruddock was himself the object of upturned and recompacted earth. Bateman claimed to have gathered first-hand, at the end of his digging arm, more information than any other grave digger ever could concerning *the primaeval sepulchres of Britain*, and perhaps he did. But look now, said the man in the hollow, look at the barrow beside me, how that man Bateman had his men dig into its centre and excavate, and tell me what this mess left over tells you about Bateman, because it tells me all I need to know, said he, and now I see how I should have come here first rather than waste an afternoon on *Ten Years' Diggings* to understand the nature of Bateman's thinking. There is no need to read *Ten Years' Diggings* in order to understand the extent of Bateman's knowledge. None need read the telling passage in which Bateman writes, *I will only add, that theory, the bane of nearly all the older Antiquarian books, has been avoided,* and that all the deductions—which are sparse indeed—as have been included herein, *are either demonstrable, or such as may be fairly inferred.* Anyone wishing to get the gist of Bateman and understand the full extent of his impoverished English outlook need merely spend time alongside one of the barrows he saw fit to ruin, almost all containing what Bateman describes as an *artless stone vault, or a stone chest, otherwise called a Kistvaen, built with more or less care, and in other cases a grave cut more or less below the natural surface, and lined, if need be, with stone slabs.* There was a lengthy pause during which the man in his hollow extended an arm—strangely long—and gathered another clod to cover himself at the midriff. Bateman claimed that all prehistoric men took to barrow raising, said he, and that when it came to the simple fact of this prolific barrow raising, this innate proclivity to raise barrows found across the globe, all peoples were related to a common stock because of it, *all men are brethren* to the extent they are derived from barrow raising ancestors. This argument, Bateman's, must be one of the more peculiar arguments I have seen for the brotherhood of man, said he in the hollow, for establishing the foundation of all universal ideas, with all universal ideas rooted in the idea of a common humanity—here derived, he continued, from the simple existence, the presumed ubiquity, of loading the dead under heavy piles of earth. This was, as I knew, an extraordinary inference for Bateman to make considering his antipathy to theory, *the bane of nearly all the older Antiquarian books*, but now not, apparently, the bane of his own. Were his outlook not so impoverished, the leap he made might have been noticed by the author himself. I have made an inference after all, he might have said. I have proposed something about our so-called brotherhood that cannot *be fairly inferred.* And I have lied a little too about that brotherhood and would rather not test my magnanimity. I have assumed a commonness, a shared humanity, in this so-called ubiquity of barrow raising. By inflating my own book, I have been drawn into inflating the significance of the barrow, as the sign of an essentialness, a proclivity, to cover the dead with heaps of stone, or earth, or muck, or sand, or whatever, so long as it is heavy. Bateman might have himself noticed it, and so noted it down. And yet, Bateman seems to prefigure the idea that when enough data is gathered, a formally massless entity gains weight, and the massing of data itself becomes its own reality and its own evaluative order. Not gathering data, not approaching the world with the gaze of an accountant, or of a bookkeeper, or collector of territories and liberties—even one so notorious as Alexander the Great who had stones heaped over his friend Hephaestion—is redefined as ignorance. In a totemic shift, the data gatherer, the heaper of evidence, becomes the guardian of knowledge and the seat of judgement. Bateman suggests that the work of his predecessor, Sir Richard Hoare, in *Ancient Wiltshire*, is next to useless *from the absence of any Craniological Notices or Measurements*. Bateman neglects to explain, said he, as if explanation were needless, how the inclusion of those craniological measurements would make the same book, *Ancient Wiltshire*, worth printing after all. Bateman presents his *List of Skulls* and his *Remarks on the Pottery of the Mounds*—each an addendum to *Ten Years' Diggings* and each an afterthought in the most literal sense—as addenda against which all subsequent volumes will be tested, and as being likely, furthermore, to establish *permanent standards of comparison in their respective classes*. That is the logic of a man like Bateman, the man in the hollow told me, and the logic of all men of our age, which holds that if something can be compared it can be judged, and it is only necessary for one thing to be positioned alongside another for its value to be assayed, and all things need only be placed in relation to other things, all moments alongside other moments, all feelings in relation to similar but not identical feelings against which they are graded, or made relational, and so made sense of. It is a horizontal thing this way of thinking, and if it has any depth, that depth is only of a depositional kind, although it mostly lacks depth and fails in its depositional concentration because this manner of thinking is eminently distractable and tends to move sideways, extending its territories by a bespattering of evidences, not knowing how or where to establish its home. That will do for Bateman, as if that would be enough to live and orient a life by, or as if a life oriented that way could proceed without eventual collapse.

The old man in the hollow could not know that Bateman's son would subsequently inherit all Bateman's things, including the loot—fragments of skulls, fragments of pots, and so on—that lay presented and outward-looking in the cabinet room of Lomberdale Hall, and how the son would sell the lot to pay for his own dissolute habits. If he could know, the old man would surely conclude that a continuous line can be traced from Bateman's logic of measurement—the placement of one thing alongside a comparable other—to his son's subsumption by the money form and its own peculiar ways of assigning and destroying value. That Bateman elevates his own peerless self upon the work of destruction is surely the truest encapsulation of his thinking, the old man in the hollow went on, given how every mound Bateman raids is another mound that cannot be investigated by a subsequent Bateman-like investigator. Bateman himself notes *the extreme improbability of any future writer having the opportunity of examining so large a collection of ancient Celtic crania and vases,* the fact of it arising, Bateman admits, *from the rapid disappearance and exhaustion of the sources of discovery*—by his very own hand, evidently, or by the pick and the shovel of the hands that Bateman hired. These hands may be unthinking as far as Bateman thought. They were those of labourers, perhaps farm hands, but they were directed hands and might be considered extensions of Bateman in that respect. Besides which, he did tend to sit close by and smoke and sketch and comment to *go on* and to stop, to scratch a little more carefully, and then to go on again as they did his digging for him. See that there logic, the man in the hollow said, and how Bateman is quick to denounce *agricultural improvements* against the example of his own destructions, and how Bateman draws attention to the havoc unguided farm hands create upon barrow-bearing land, all of it for not scratching carefully when told, for not having Bateman to tell them. And so too does he lament the *ill-conducted pillage of idle curiosity,* against which his own well-conducted pillage is to be—again—measured.

Whereas Thomas Browne inspected those urns that were turned up by accident and remained spectating as others were dug out, Thomas Bateman took destruction before sense and then measured himself well because of it, said the man in the hollow, un-holding a book by Browne in one hand, as he said so, and a book by the—as yet unborn—Argentine in the other.

§

When in 1658 Mr. Dugdale wrote Browne of his hopes to *procure one of those large heaps of earth to be cut through, to the end, that we may see whither any urnes or other things of note are covered therewith,* he receives no reply from Browne—already now renowned for his urn interest. Or at least, Mr. Dugdale receives no reply on this specific of the mound and its digging. Browne addresses other matters instead in letters subsequent that month. But the doctor did reply, said the man in the hollow,

87

and Browne buried that reply in a letter he sent almost a year later. *But manie things prove obscure in subterraneous discoverie,* the relevant paragraph begins. Browne goes on to note several pregnant examples, before finishing on the most exemplary case of the ox-wrapped corpse.

—About 5 yeares agoe an humerous man of this countrie, after his death and according to his owne desire, was wrap't up in the horned hide of an oxe, & so buried —

Do not dig then overly seriously, or with too much mechanical diligence of the mind, Browne effectively says here, said he, for in this instance I relate, *when the memorie hereof is past, how this may hereafter confound the discoverers.* They will wonder to see a man wrapped up in the horned hide of the ox, as if that meant something more than nothing, or something beyond the extent of his prank.

—what conjectures may arise thereof, it is not easie to conjecture, but all conjecture in this case will be a consequence of the hoax. So do not over dig at problems like these, Mr. Dugdale, and gather your intelligence from books, or at least books written by serious-minded people, and from dissection, in the case of a doctor, that is to say from bodies which can no longer joke.

§

Thomas Browne, said he in the hollow, was faced with the prospect of numerous urns that might well be found anywhere the Romans settled, it seemed, because they were turned up everywhere, and would, he speculated, remain impossible to count. Their eventual number could only be guessed at given how many ancients have died, how the dead outnumber the living, and how comparatively easy it was for them to burn the body and stuff a few ashes and unburnt teeth in a jar and place that jar in a pit in the ground. By contrast, Thomas Bateman's mounds of earth, his stone tombs, his ancient barrows, these were always limited in number, they were harder to produce, and so it was that Thomas Bateman had it in his power to ensure the barrows, or a good proportion of them, were wiped clean of their remains in the wake of his picking—the collector's passion. The destruction caused, as each barrow was transformed into a form of archaeological landfill, was not taken as fit for reflection, nor for any kind of discussion in *Ten Years' Diggings*—Bateman does not explain how each trench was backfilled—and the process is only mentioned by way of a joke Mr. Bateman makes at the expense of Mrs. Bateman, who, as they were refilling an excavation in Monsal Dale, *had the misfortune to drop in, unobserved, a gold ring set with an onyx cameo.* This former gift, most probably from her husband, represented *a classical subject,* and its dropping and subsumption by the witless infilling of Bateman's hired hands was *an occurrence* of no small amusement to Mr. Bateman, if not so much to Mrs. Bateman. Its re-emergence, Bateman writes, *may some day lead to the conclusion that the Romans buried in these ancient grave-hills,* which they did not. And so, whilst Thomas Browne saw how a joke might make a mockery of digging, Thomas Bateman failed to see how an accident made a mockery not of his wife, but his own entire project. And whilst Thomas Browne saw how the world of men was busy annihilating itself and needed no further help, Thomas Bateman placed himself on the side of the annihilators and recapitulated every burial he could discover, digging fresh trenches that were filled once he was done with his upturned muck. Or that, at least, was the gist of what the old man said against Bateman, and in favour of Browne, for knowing of Bateman myself—his *Ten Years' Diggings* is in the wall too, of course—and having read Browne, it was evident to me that this is what the old man in his hollow would think, a man who was more preoccupied with clawing his hand at his own clods and gathering the dirt to himself, a superior investigation of the mound, so he said.

§

Some mounds were really rather large and took more digging at. The barrow known as Gib Hill was got at by William Bateman in 1824 when Thomas Bateman, his son, was still very small and probably only just learning how not to stick all things he encountered in his mouth. Not much was found at that first dig—a small iron fibula, a dart or javelin point of flint, a battered celt of basaltic stone—and it was left to the son in 1848, now a man who knew the use of his mouth, to resume the activity of digging, which meant ordering others where to set about it.

January 10th was occupied in removing the upper part of the hill, writes Bateman, Jr. This was done by way of the usual trench and in the cut already established by his father. A few splinters of animal bone and a single flake of calcined flint were the product of the day. The labourers lodged at a nearby inn. Bateman took a carriage back to Lomberdale Hall, a short trot to the east. It was a Monday.

January 11th. Further trenching of the barrow taking the cut beyond the mid-point at its apex. Due to the size of the mound this trench did not extend to the base yet and thereby cut the mound in two, but remained curiously raised. It yielded that day a dog's tooth, several animal bones, more calcined flakes of flint, and a neatly formed arrowhead of the same material. The labourers went back to the inn and picked at their fingernails whilst saying various things, none of them favourable, about Bateman. They nicknamed the barrow the cracked nipple, one of their number having seen such a thing and declaring the likeness. For his part, Bateman decided to walk back to Lomberdale Hall sending the carriage ahead without him so that he could scheme and plot how they would expend their energies on the 12th.

January 12th. The trench was widened around the centre of the barrow at its apex, which led to various innuendos about the cracked nipple that Bateman could not follow. A layer of tempered earth approaching the consistency of hard clay, some loose stones, a fragment of an urn, and more chippings of flint were those things that Bateman noted.

January 13th. The trench was deepened, digging through the before-named clay and layers of decomposed wood and charcoal—the surviving bark suggested hazelwood. The cut they had made still remained some feet at its base from the undisturbed earth, or the ground as it originally was before the barrow raisers heaped clods and stones and rubble all over it many hundreds or several thousands of years before. More animal bones and flints, *one of the latter being a fine instrument of semi-circular shape,* notes Bateman—which was Bateman's attempt at seeing something worthwhile in what was dug. It rained intermittently—an extraordinary thought, this, that wet, dreary days like that occurred in the mid-nineteenth century, just as they did in the mid-eighteenth, and mid-twentieth, and so on, and that wet, dreary days, had been suffered in this part of the world by all sorts of people engaged in all sorts of tasks which had them endure it as Bateman's labourers did. This was also the day the innuendos stopped and distaste for Bateman set in and could no longer be judged an evening pastime.

January 14th. The barrow trench was finally dug down all the way to the undisturbed earth. It measured 25 feet by 18, and 15 feet in height at its highest point—that point being the barrow apex such as still existed. From what he saw of the stuff they turned over and out, Bateman decided the barrow was built over four original mounds of indurated clay mixed with wood and charcoal, and was, therefore, a less than typical monument. The superimposed materials of the subsequent mound were of a *looser description*, wrote Bateman. These materials are of a *looser description*, he told his men who felt those materials had been dense enough to dig at and had Bateman himself dug at them this gent might have described the underlying mounds differently, as *even much worse to dig at*, for instance, or, less politely, as *truly shit-awful dirt*—or whatever mid-nineteenth century expletive might have been appropriate to the context—and would, in turn, have designated the overlaying mound as not quite as bad to dig at but still awful enough—that is, Bateman would have defined all materials excavated according to some negation or other, and his entire account of the mound would have been negative in all its inflexions. When Bateman was not standing over them, giving commentary and looking for objects to collect from their spoil, this Bateman sat with a little tray of discovered artefacts, more flints as usual—he only pretended interest at these now—a round instrument of some sort which preoccupied him greatly, and some large, disconnected bones of oxen, he thought, all very much decayed. Bateman took the carriage back to Lomberdale Hall that afternoon feeling a trifle defeated and fatigued by his disappointments.

January 15th. It was resolved by Bateman that a tunnel would be driven into the mound from the west. This would penetrate the barrow at right-angles to the trench they had cut it in two. After three or four yards tunnelling it was deemed unsafe and the men would go no further, and to prove the point, knocked the supporting timbers and watched with satisfaction as the entire superstructure fell in. Bateman was also satisfied, not by the collapsing—he felt his men held strange notions of proof—but from what the collapse revealed. The internment was finally located, not at the base of the mound, as is usual, but suspended in the earth near its top. *This consisted of a rectangular cist,* wrote Bateman, *measuring inside 2 feet by 6 inches by 2 feet, composed of four massive blocks of limestone, covered in by a fifth of irregular form, averaging 4 feet square by 10 inches thick.* This cap stone was not 18 inches *beneath the turf clothing the summit, and in fact the men had been working directly under the cist for some time.* These particulars were only subsequently assembled, given how, as soon as the cist was discovered, the sides of it collapsed, and a very pretty vase was revealed just as it was crushed to pieces, the vase-fragments *mingling with the burnt human bones in company with which it had for ages occupied the sepulchral chamber.* This type of urn, writes Bateman, was no cinerary urn, and would never have been stuffed with human remains. It was of the sort that might have contained food or drink. Another of those artefacts that pre-historic peoples saw fit to have *indifferently deposited*, as Bateman phrases it—which means, its presence there, in the cist, made no sense to Bateman at all, who nonetheless had the vase restored almost to original perfection, so he claimed. With the vase in a box, and the bones left behind, Bateman directed his men to the last task of the day, to load the cist in its separate blocks onto a cart and follow him back to Lomberdale Hall where the cist would subsequently be re-assembled in the garden, and would look more like an altar, or perhaps more appropriately, a small seat, or bird table, than a cist.

January 16th. No digging. It was a Sunday.

January 17th. A molar tooth from the lower jaw of a horse—retrieved from some of the rubbish which fell out of the cist on the Saturday just gone. This was done by Bateman alone, picking among all the mess they had created. The men were paid off and dispersed back to their previous employments in and about the town of Middleton.

Cist of Gib Hill Tumulus.

Whilst gathering the bones of the small rodent-like animals that had roved the flat and died and become desiccated there, I was reminded of the flying serpents mentioned by Herodotus that lay piled at the mountain pass. Somehow, I imagined those flying serpents lay complete, just as skeletons are reconstructed and hung in natural history museums, although some skeletons prepare themselves for the requisite connexion and rigidity in life. This was the nature of a skeleton Bateman mentions, only mentions, barely described like most dug by Bateman and his men, excepting one peculiarity, the connexion of two lumbar vertebrae, *attached together by an abnormal growth of osseous substance.*

The flat before the wall is hostile to any kind of burial. The ground is almost entirely solid and there are no small particles to speak of that might be blown across it. Or if there are particles, they do not gather, for there are no small hollows where the wind is slack and they might drop and accumulate. There could be no place further removed from the land of tumuli, I thought at the time, where persons interred include *a female in the prime of life, and a child of about four years of age,* the former on her left side with her knees drawn up, the child placed above her *and rather behind her shoulders.* Determined not to theorise this or any other detail, Bateman does not ask why the female, possibly the child's mother, is so indifferently arranged, and why the two of them have only the comfort of their own foetal positioning. This might be a gross translocation of sentiment, and perhaps, indeed, Bateman's unsentimental report of their arrangement is the only advantage of his own breed of indifference. Bateman moves instead to describe the bones that surround and cover them, those of the water-vole, or rat, and the presence of a cow's tooth. Still more words are expended upon the necklace of jet worn by the woman, how many beads are thin laminae, how many cylindrical, how many conical. Her skull is described—*beautiful in its proportions*—and so, gross sentiment survives after all. It has been chosen to appear *in the Crania Britannica as the type of the ancient British female.* Her femur measures 15 and half inches.

The presence of rats' bones is so common in cist burials that Bateman remarks when they are absent, *the usual layer of rats' bones was absent.* Absence itself is measured in rat's bones — *having removed these materials without meeting with anything more important than rat's bones.* And so too is plenitude —*as large an accumulation of the bones of the water-vole as we have seen in any barrow.* And moderation —*here were many rats' bones but not in the profusion sometimes met with.*

Another barrow, another body or more—we found a skeleton; two skeletons; at least two skeletons; three skeletons; the skeleton of a child without relics; the skeleton of a young person laid on the ribs of an ox; a skeleton wanting the head; a double interment with the adult below the infant, a few months old; the imperfect remains of four persons; at least three adults and one child; two infants and an adult so huddled together as to make them near indistinguishable; four adult skeletons—these might have been disturbed before we dug at them ourselves; numerous skeletal parts beneath a submerged floor that *abounded with rats' bones*—the human remains had evidently *been drawn beneath it by these restless creatures*; twelve skeletons ranging from infancy to senility; twelve skeletons mostly exhibiting the lengthened form of the skull seen in previous skeletons; at least thirteen individuals of all ages including females; fifteen skeletons laid upon each other without much arrangement although their skulls, for the most part, faced east; an indeterminate number of individuals from infants to adults of large stature, all in a state of disorder bar one; the skeleton of a boy with a small pebble found in the right hand; the skeleton of a second found due to the appearance of its feet beside the first; the skeleton of a very young woman; the skeleton of a tall man; of a middle aged man, and another, and another; we found some *broken human bones accompanied by those of the rat*; two phalanges of a human finger alongside the lower jaw of a large quadruped—rubbed down, and *a few portions of the skeleton of a child* together with *a few bones from the extremities of a fully grown person*. The skeleton of a recent burial was also found in a barrow. Upon consulting two aged persons living in the neighbourhood, it was determined as the body of Francis Brown, found hung, and buried as a suicide, though two criminals executed at York some years later confessed to the killing of poor Brown, and to making it look that way by hanging the body and kicking a stool below it. The remainder of the barrow contained the usual fare, but including *a round piece of ruddle, or red war paint*. We found traces of former occupants in nothing more than the shape of human teeth and, as definitive evidence, the bones of the rat. In another only rats' bones— alone proof of the mound's sepulchral nature; we saw bones laid *in every direction* and bones *in the utmost confusion* and pieces of human bone burnt and unburnt; we found a skeleton so broken up none of the long bones could be measured, and *a few fragments of calcined bone too minute to be assigned either to a human or animal subject,* and bones so decayed they had *almost reached the inevitable catastrophe* of becoming dust. We saw a bone of rhomboidal shape; a third skeleton which faced the first; a second skeleton which lay on the fourth; a fifth skeleton mingled with the second, and so on; the remains of an infant buried alongside more significant others and of an infant entirely on its own and unaccompanied by anything of interest; a barrow containing *calcined human bones lying in the very spot where they had been drawn together while the embers of the funeral pyre were glowing;* a skeleton surrounded by rats' bones, all partially charred by the subsequent burning of a neighbouring corpse—*the rats must have resorted for many generations to the place previous to their becoming blackened by the fire;* a corpse buried when the grave and surrounding stones were still hot; a barrow containing only burnt bones and no artefacts—a barrow that upon closer inspection, a kind Bateman does not give, might well yield evidence of *suttee, and infanticide, both which abominations we are unwillingly compelled by accumulated evidence to believe were practised in Pagan Britain;* a burned infant; an unburned infant; the remains of a young female and a female by whose face were the *indications—* remains—*of a very young child;* of two human bodies—one of them calcined; of a man; of a woman; one with the head facing east, to the south-west, to the west south-west, to the south, the south-east, and so on, including the north-east, and once even the north-west—indicating all points of the compass had especial significance, or that orientation meant nothing; hands

on thighs, or where the thighs would have been, and hands to
the face; a group with bone-tipped weapons owning to their
ignorance of metal; *remains of a child of tender age around which
were*—again—*numerous rats' bones*; of a man in the prime of
life; of a skeleton subsequently displayed in a glass case at
Lomberdale; of a skeleton *the consistency of cheese*; of an aged
man with a short round cranium placed in a heap with the skull
on top; of a man with a very fine cranium and *a portion of the
cranium of another subject*; of an infant with only a fragment of
the skull remaining and no other bones; of two small jawless
crania placed side by side near a drinking cup; of a child with
an abnormal skull—signs of hydrocephalus; of a woman of
small stature and with a remarkably small and flattened skull—
possibly by artificial compression in youth; of a skull flattened
at the back, and another, and another, indeed so often seen it
*may be attributed to some prevailing method of nursing during
infancy* for the ancient Briton; of a skull robbed of its teeth prior
to our visit; of a skull much distorted and flattened by pressure;
of a skull containing an arrowhead; of a skull of the boat-shaped
type; of another skull of the boat-shaped type; of a skull
fragment which had been removed from another place, and a
skull with wide maxillaries, a retreating forehead, and the frontal
sinuses prominent, as well as a skull best described as *globular*;
of an adult with a mass of osseous substance protruding on a
portion of the jaw; of an aged person with a repaired leg fracture
just above the ankle; of a man with both bones of the left leg
broken and re-joined; of a man with one broken femur firmly
reunited so as to shorten the leg; of a man with two deformed
femurs; *of a full sized person who had suffered from a morbid
enlargement of the head of the right humerus*; of a man with

fractured and re-joined nasal bones; of a man with a skull of 74 and a half ounces capacity; of an aged man with a skull of 80 ounces and many teeth wanting, the rest severely worn; of a skull containing cricoid cartilage conveyed inside by a hibernating rat; of an unusually thick skull accompanied by the usual rats' bones; of a skull considered to be *a typical example of the brachy-cephalic variety of the Ancient British head*; of a skull with unusually rugged facial features; of a man with the skull rotted at the side where it rested against earth; of several other skulls rotted in the exact same way; of several bodies of two distinct internments; of three distinct internments and one containing *bones of about six individuals* and another *three or four persons*; of a female occupying the space left vacant by the previous tenant—his bones gathered up and placed below a nearby slab; of a very slender skeleton buried in a slovenly manner; of a skeleton whose bones indicated a hasty burial, and so on and etcetera. Some were found in a mound hitherto untouched; or in a setting much rifled and mutilated by barrow-robbers, treasure-seekers, and stone-getters; or in the garden of a lady; or in a mound already part-excavated by a predecessor; in a barrow dug *after repeated disappointments*; in earth that *emitted an odour so fragrant as to cause us to look see whether there were not many flowers close by*—there were none; at a site excavated to its last by candlelight and reached after a very long and cold drive through a mountainous country; in a mound near a chasm *formerly considered unfathomable*; and a mound *quite overlooked till the previous day when it was noticed while shooting*; and finally, one named after an unearthly or supernatural being much feared in remote villages—*a curious instance of the inherent tendency of the mind to assign a reason to everything uncommon or unaccountable which no extent of ignorance or apathy seems able totally to eradicate.* But so too was dug a hill *wrapped in as much mystery as ever*—there being no remains of any sort, and certainly no fragments of bone, nor the briefest wish of a skeleton in the contracted posture, knees drawn up, lying on the left side as usual. This was the flexed position of all barrow internments, excepting those where the bones were buried as a pile, or reduced to ash, or non-existent, and excepting the tall man who lay on his back but with his head facing west, and another that was not described as tall but was considered powerful, and another almost completely decayed but with the head again facing west, or the man who lay straight with his head on a slab for a pillow—it turned out to be the lid of a cist containing an infant, or the man who lay outstretched with his hands on his thighs, or the man who lay with finger bones in the hollow of the pelvis, or the two found in a line, or the five laid side by side—none of them Christians, no evidence of coffins—or the middle aged man who lay knees drawn up on his right side—contrary to the usual custom—as well as the aged man, again on his right and with his knees drawn up so as to nearly touch the face, and so too the two found facing one another, one slim, the other robust, both with their knees drawn up, then the same again but with the skulls touching, and so on, as well as every skeleton that had been disturbed and thrown about previous, some with a sprinkling of chippings, one with *shapeless pieces of melted glass* and another with a blue glass bead—a spiral thread of white running through it, one with a chunk of haematite, another with a polecat's skull, and then one with the lower mandible of a hawk, yet another interred beside two vases which *contained nothing but fine mould,* a small brass coin of Tetricus the elder *which had probably slipped from near the top of the barrow through the interstices of the stones,* and so many with daggers, and pots, and ashes, and horns, and the odd horse's tooth, and so on and again including a swine's tooth, almost all still *amidst myriads of water rats' bones,* or *an enormous quantity of rats' bones,* or *masses of rats' bones* and *great quantities of rats' bones* and *numerous rats' bones,* and to vary it, *plentifully mingled with rats' bones around the skeleton,* or *a skeleton completely embedded in rats' bones,* or again, *alongside and under many bones of the water-vole.* So much for the land of tumuli.

§

To the east of the turnpike road is an old encampment walled with stones large as strong gate stoops, some a ton apiece. No engines now in operation could move them. Nearby another ancient wall, neolithic one might think, except here the blocks are ten tons or more and are piled lengthways to defend against passage up the hill or at least give those walking up something to think over. But visitors might very well have been distracted by the sight of a prodigious logan, or DRUIDICAL ROCKING-STONE, just up the rise from the fort. It is said to rock from the pressure of a palm, or shoulder, but not a finger, though I did not try it, writes Bateman.

§

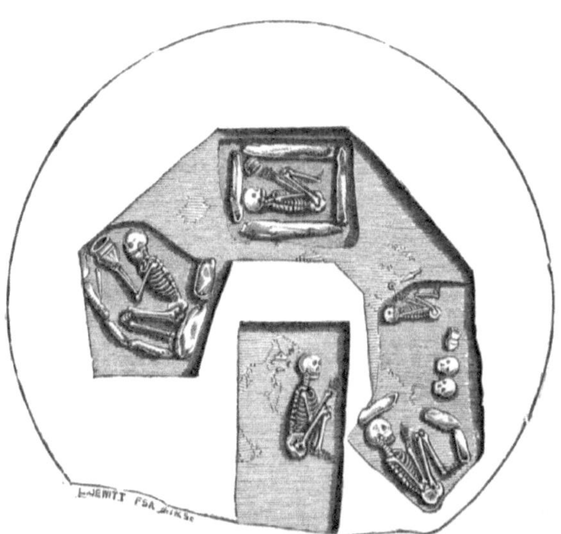

Plan of Barrow near Monsal Dale.

§

Tracing down over rocky outcrops, I looked at each foothold and thought over, and perhaps also despite them—*these here, highest contusions of the earth, can only themselves diminish with time.* They must weather back and the mountain will itself shorten. It was how I reckoned against this last massif, or found myself reckoning, seeking to set myself above in geological time, doing so unthinkingly, reasoning with and recollecting fragments of knowledges and applying them with due whimsy, this typical and typifying feature of a mind clocking over as the rest of me kept with the descending to that part of the decline, the one new to me then, where the first spoil heaps appear in the last and leeward territory of the nomads.

Each outward growing spoil heap, formed by discarded rock fell over its edge, was either by or right near below its adit. This hole in the mountainside, rarely above shoulder height, gives to a low, crouching, and bitten-out corridor going inwards to the mine, more than usually wet, and progressing in defiance of the brute solemnity of the peak. The sun this day lay heavy and dry, and the last sip of water rolled across my tongue and was gone with it. They stood by the entrances to these little VENTICULES, as I was to call them then, and blocked my going in to lick at the walls or open my mouth to each dripping ceiling. All that was left over for me, as they stood there blocking, were the last breath reaches of subterranean air, cool as a wintry draft and sufficient to raise the skin in bumps as though freshly plucked and readied for the oven. Every adit on this side of the mountain did breathe out that way, exhaling the frigid internal lung of abandoned bronchioles with their multiple chambers and shafts and tunnels chasing the depleted seams and ore. Coming down this way with a thirst that was somehow still less than my aversion to their company, I skirted each spoil heap, and did not interrupt their standing, knowing, or perhaps it was simply that I hoped this would be the final time I saw the nomads. They were uncomprehending in their standing, paused in their wandering. Outward facing, the frigid air at their backs, stood silent before their respective adit, and so plainly not looking at the evidences of earlier extraction. In the scheme of plunder this had only been a temporary recruitment by those below of the higher lands. Otherwise these regions and others like them were mostly left aside, viewed from their foothills as impediments to travel, or, when really stared at, were felt to be *the sign of indifference* to a grand scale. Even if mountains do figure in ancient myth and thinking and take some room in the imaginary both then and subsequently, this is nothing in proportion to their stature, their mass, their unthinkable physicality, and so indeed, their tendency as they are climbed to grow and divulge only further mute faces of themselves across their unavailing yet forever changing aspect. In many respects a reflection of and so companion to the sea, although the ocean arrays its unreachable extent quite simply by the laying of a surface between air and liquid, a surface that can be penetrated by a massed object, but not followed without becoming inert and unfeeling oneself. Whereas mountain terrain tends to flatter its distant onlooker and the occasional visitor with the impression that it has been seen. There is most often little or no ingress below the exterior, although even when a mountain is full of holes, the landform is still treated as raised surface and is not thought in terms of its inner mass, nor is it understood in terms of the crust of the planet from which it extrudes. This reduction is one that, in the last, no mountain can truly allow, which is why each changes shape as it is approached, subsequently climbed, and finally conquered. Those who claim a peak presume to claim its highest declivity, failing as they descend to notice how the mountain builds up and transforms behind their preoccupied retreat. This the nomads did most likely understand, which would make their standing by each abandoned mine a savouring of the substance of their host. So it was that I left the mountain, and arrived at the single only place on earth which is pure surface—the flat.

§

In the region of the flat before the wall no large animals live and so no large skins may be gathered at ground level. There are plentiful skins, however, at a height of some 25 to 30 feet above the ground. Here is the first intermittent layer to which the lowest skins descend, with others at 50 feet or more forming a secondary layer that was beyond reach of my implements. They resembled clouds in their movements—only much closer and smaller—the lower layer moving against the upper, and at times they amassed, at others they dispersed, and for large parts of the flat were so sparse in their arrangement that the ground was only infrequently mottled by their passing. Resolving to build a balloon I paid these skins more attention. The small grappling hook I carried was tied to my pack, bound upturned, and had become, so I saw, coated at each point with rust. These points had been grazed by rock in the mountains and so the metal exposed along each elemental tear to the ingress of air, moisture, and atomic rot. I resort to the grappling hook rarely yet always to a situation of utter dependence. Using the hook involves a necessary death of the will, or perhaps better put, it requires an abdication of the self before the arrival of a raw but serene fatalism. Or this was how I figured it. With lesser words admittedly. My state of abjection, as I would subsequently write, held out below the decision of what can only be described as fatal caprice, I should call it that, which was the elemental chance of the hook to hold in position or fail in that holding on rock, in a crevice. Its decision was no longer my own to manipulate in my favour, which is how it relied upon a temporary killing of the self, as said. Where the hook found purchase, that purchase decided. This dependence stole my sense of trust, or faith, and replaced it with the nothingness of not knowing if what was needed would give. This nothingness was not merely about not knowing but about having no means to persuade the elements against failure, or reposition the hook, and alter my chances of survival. Regular climbers are probably so habituated to the nothingness beyond each unalterable decision that these words no longer make sense to them, and so they return to words like faith, and belief, even though such words have no application here. For my part, this sensation came to me still in its novelty, as a consequence of each decision to climb, or descend, when scaling the otherwise insurmountable, or when I lowered myself into the valleys. I came like this to come down into those shaped like an ear on either side of the ridge, and which recalled too, to my mind, the stone ears built into the walls of Ancient Egypt, set waiting, listening there for prayers and whispers to the gods. Of all the letters this valley shape most closely resembled the letter G of my own alphabet. As each valley curled inwards from the outer helix to the tragus, it terminated in a deep pit where some fell, others were thrown, and still others talked and shouted into the abyss, seeking to stir as I thought the neural pathways of an unknowable, subterranean realm. In any case, from the ridge it looked set to repeat.

GGGGGGGGGGGGG
ƆƆƆƆƆƆƆƆƆƆƆƆƆ

But to return to the skins which floated above, forming two horizons in the sky of the flat and resembling autumn leaves layered in a stagnant yet recently stirred pond, I attached my rope to the loop and threw back the hook and the trail of it into the air. The lowest skins were the only ones I could reach and these hardly even. Most throws I would manage to get the hook 20 feet into the air or thereabouts, and needed to rest my throwing arm before resolving to attempt another casting up of the hook and line. It caused a severe ache about the shoulder, in the socket. When restored I would occasionally throw well, but the angle was wrong. It is surely difficult to throw both vertical and hard rather than just vertical or just hard. If the hook contacted a skin at the rim but did not hole it or move it down by some particle, merely the skin would be pushed aside and buffet its neighbour, each skin neither gaining altitude nor losing it and hardly tilting from its level plane. This seemed to me a sign of their neutrality in relation to most forces, or at least, an indication that the skins were indifferently possessed as they mustered together and floated away to darken another part of the flat. But when the hook fell over the edge it need not even perforate the skin to bring it downwards, simply the act of crumpling and thereby bringing a section of the skin below its plane would take the rest with it, flapping to the ground. When my throwing arm was done for, I lay on my back and made small eddy currents with a stick. Not so much a suckhole but an ascending vortex, a thread of air first wound from the end of the rod, imperceptible at that point, even against whetted lips, but this imperceptible nothing gathered circumference and strengthened as it resolved upwards. The skins at 25 feet shifted reluctantly against their inertias but ultimately irresistibly against mine and began to jostle and rotate and divert to the first rumour of a shadow arc. At 50 feet and over where the vortex had further extended, they began to submit more definitely, and as the winds of the flat took them north and so out of the scope of my reach, they spun sideways.

The motion of skins is unrelatable to most and has only occurred in this part of my travels, and not prior, and certainly not where I was born, or where I first had cause to walk. The land was still parcelled up and largely enclosed.

§

Walking east I met a man. Said he was busy with getting a stone for a gate to hang from or clap to. Said too he could not go to his usual place. This when I still met with all sorts of people who said various things. Some said far more than others, of course, being in the habit of saying, and not so much with hefting, or being in the habit of thinking that saying was hefting, more likely.

§

He said, I could hear the ending of sentences already mid-way through, if not as they opened, and that anyone who becomes sensitive to grammar will hear it just as well, first in speech as the speaker prepares their voice for the descent of the sentence to its endpoint, and then with the text, even telegrammic text, or text as it is in the process of being typed that is without the inflexions of the voice but is clearly enough preparing for the coming pause, some would call it a breath, a breather, but he saw in it the acknowledgement—unknowing, irresistible—of oblivion, a pause found just as much and somehow worse in punctuation marks, although these are more definite and irruptive on the page than in speech.

He said that he walked with another along a shallow sea, creatures brushing at their feet, and heard him tell of a book he was writing across languages—Danish, French and English— no sentence containing one language, or hardly any, and that he attempted a kind of improvised Urdu at times, and that he was painting upon an enormous canvas a detail for the front cover—the ibex in its dominion—which somehow I saw even as we waded and reached the shore where five millipedes lay dead, recently dredged from the sediment, each the width of a thigh and the weight of a hawser. He said every image is a contrived image and that the book he was writing would do away with the lot of them, that the ibex would be his last, and it too was an indulgence, and he was already embarrassed by it, and there would not be a single insect or hawser in sight.

§

He told me that asking the question, why I write, is one he rarely posed to himself because I found the lack of a proper answer difficult, so he said, although one justification I attempt and then dispense with—because I do not wish to solidify it—is to write against this everywhere increasingly shut off by a kind of endemic decay, a sort of over-determined or pre-ordained degeneration that appears to be occurring at all levels, from body, to society, to lifeworld. And that this holding or fabrication of spaces, of suspended moments in writing, can only be done by acts of erasure and negativity tenderly disposed which are at the same time acts of recollection, or reconstruction, by a kind of layman's belligerence within the carapace of the scholar.

He said that erasure would be his hope if he did not avoid the word. And that in writing he liked to think we are not after all doomed to living out our histories and to being all this all that has made us in ever more grotesque forms, which seems, said he, to be exactly what we are doing.

§

He said of books there are two options worth considering, and these are not mutually exclusive. First, that the book— book writing, book printing, book consumption—might be considered to be one of the last reflexes of an ailing culture, a culture in its death throes, a bookish reflex that is flexing still, and might be understood as a kind of death tremor or Lazarus sign. Second, that the book, and all it involves—the desire to write one before all else—is a kind of disease, or another marker of a diseased state, a terminal condition, a specific form of suffering that is also a mechanism of distraction, of inaction and paralysis.

§

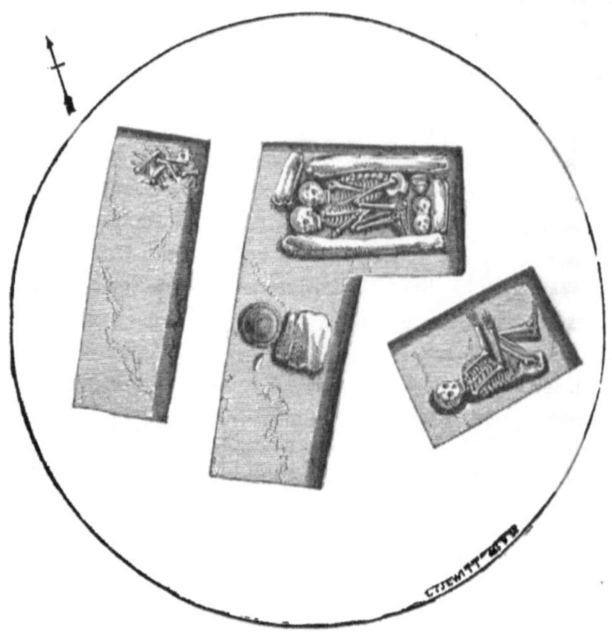

Plan of a Barrow near Monsal Dale.

§

And that there were traces of fern embossed, in a way, upon the verdigris that grew outwards as the dagger expanded by its oxidant. So too, handfuls could be found in high rot around the bones from head to foot, not frondescent, or brown, but almost pitch as dead plants go. It is certain, Bateman writes, these ferns were first placed as a couch to receive the body, and that further leaves were subsequently laid over the whole of it to protect from the earth. There is no speculation nor surprise at the survival of the ferns whilst the skeleton itself was all that remained of the body, the soft parts long corrupted and vanished from sight. The emplacement of the weapons is recorded as a script upon the corpse, these having sunken as the fleshy parts reduced, came to rest against bone, and being bronze, coloured it green.

§

The copperplate engraving and the woodcut gives the pen of the artist its widest circulation, just as moveable type does for the scribe. But this is their only association. Engravers relate to the pen more or less directly. The burin—the engraver's instrument—is not dissimilar from a pen and cuts a groove for the ink to fill. And just as the pen pressed hard thickens its own delivery, the size of the burin's cut is proportional to the amount of ink that can be transferred by it.

The page waiting for the pen to mark some of it but leave most of it blank is like the unscored metal plate in anticipation of the burin—both will not be inked where they are left untouched—the plate because it retains no ink on the polished parts, the page because the pen will not touch its white spaces, or cannot touch them, or not all of them, if the other lines of the pen are to retain definition. All of which means that a pen can more or less draft or prefigure what the burin excavates from the copperplate, it can more or less anticipate how the burin will need to move.

This relationship the woodcut inverts as it shifts from penmanship to xylographic sign. It is the uncut, higher plane

113

of the wood that transfers the ink, with the original blank woodblock surface reduced gradually to narrow ridges or larger but isolated expanses. The lines of the woodcut are not made by striking along. Each plateau or ridgeline is created bilaterally, trilaterally, and so on—from the gouging out. They are liberated from the wood as territories are slowly dug from either side, never to be attended in themselves, but left raw. Only a certain depth of the cut, or the pit, or the valley, is necessary to form the ridge, and reaching the necessary depth is the woodcutter's sole object. These areas might resemble territories seen and unseen and would never be noticed. The specific ridge and furrow patterning of the neighbouring land will appear—each furrow in its minutest detail. The nearby valleys known to the woodcutter since childhood will have been cut at least once if only roughly on some woodblock, somewhere. The bend of the river where the swing rope hung. And surely each quarry in the region, both abandoned and those still being dug, were gouged out of the pulp. The floor of a nearby lake never yet dredged nor known will take form in the woodblock, and the as yet unmapped oceanic trench will be found there too, just as every extra-terrestrial landform must be rendered at some point. It is a surety of the medium, with so many thrusts made from so many angles, and with so much infinitesimal detail a consequence, that even something as distant and unknown as the surfaces of the hard planets will have been mapped, though in fragments, yet in all their morphological peculiarity, and other planetary systems from nearby stars will have been made too, in minute prescription, insofar as these stars tether solid wanderers and not merely gaseous ones. The lunar maria must have been cut and would have been identifiable, should anyone have looked. On the earthward side these plains are sufficiently distant yet still known, and, in principle, would be identifiable in the wood. The *Mare Crisium*—the sea of crisis, just visible from Earth with the naked eye should have been dug if only once, or the elevated lake, the *Mare Spumans* or foaming sea, again on the near side, or the sea of moisture which buds from the ocean of storms—where the Copernicans reside—or the *Mare Frigoris*—the sea of cold towards the north of the moon. Even the far side of the moon, much pitted, more rugged, and never visible from the earth, has been crudely depicted in the cut-out regions of several woodcut blocks dating from the seventeenth century and subsequently lost. The far side has fewer low-lying regions, and so this happenstance might be easier to believe. Altogether, all known and unknown formations were to be found in almost every major detail and sometimes with specific accuracy on at least one block, only these woodcuts were never viewed in respect of those parts. They depicted other celestial trenches too, the Martian *Valles Marineris* in its entirety, as well as the dunes of Pluto, and many other as yet unclassified formations destined perhaps to be forever unknown to exogeology, a science not yet invented. Had they been seen, and perhaps they were in an idle moment—the seventeenth century was surely full of these like any other—they could not yet resemble those dunes of Pluto, of course, or the Mariner Valley, or the far side of the moon, to take just three, since these were not yet recognisable formations and would remain largely unknown even when they were. And yet, if the woodcutter had inverted their looking, something beyond earth would have been touched by their sight. Or at least, nobody could claim thereafter to have seen the *Valles Marineris* for the first time.

But the fate of the woodcut was not this, none of the recessed details held any kind of significance, and so they scarcely existed. The fibres of the block torn up from their first settling in at the ring—a matter of indifference. There is no image in the lower contours of those regions that transfer no ink, even though they are filled with their own infinitesimal originals arising from the score.

The process of woodcutting with the various instruments—gougers of different gauges—gives to a certain transformation of the line. There can be no perfect fidelity to the design sketch that precedes the woodcut. No single penned line is left unaltered. All must be approximated by a completely different mechanism of line production. Initially conceived as an easy stroke, its cutting requires multiple movements of the gougers, defining the ridges by a thousand strokes from the valleys that do not signify beyond their void achievement. And hence, whilst the burin or the pen defines the line by deliberate and direct inscription, the woodcut produces a line by the creation of absences, or declivities. Its minimum width is conditioned by practical factors such as the nature of the wood itself, and the pressure each ridgeline or peak must withstand during the process of printing. Too thin, or feeble, and the woodcut image will decay as it is inked and pressed. Which explains the tendency of the woodcut to a directness of statement, a roughness, if not an essential crudity, and a certain kind of independence from the intentions of a hand that must, ultimately, make do with the end result, what remains from the chipping.

The task of the woodcutter when faced with a pen-drawn image is to crystallise the irregular patterns of searching lines, and firm up all so-called organic gestures, by seeking out and voiding those lozenges of white that are correlative of their interlacing activity.

The continuous line of the pen is ultimately disregarded, and the cutter works at the level of the fragment, producing a pitted mosaic, fields of erupted tesserae—each a novel absolute.

A weave of cross-drawn lines is produced by gouging square or rhomboid pits, hatchings by digging parallel trenches, and curves by hacking arched beaches and deeps. The knife, the chisel, these are wielded from multiple angles, with innumerable thrusts, against the printable parts of the block.

All of which would be hidden by those seeking to perfect the woodcut. Efforts were at least made in that direction by the mechanically minded cutter. Those who sought to perfect the woodcut, these so-called perfectionists, would seek to obliterate the very qualities which made it distinct. The function of the woodcut begins to approximate that of the reproductive engraving which becomes its master form. When viewing those perfected or apparently perfected woodcuts, these woodcuts resembling engravings, some effort is required to understand the inversions under which they were still produced. Or, alternatively, the perfected woodcut might be considered a corruption, and the observer might stay awhile longer with the woodcut in its more expressive and basic form.

Still none could say of the woodcutter as they have said of the artist in other contexts—drawn, painted, engraved—that the cutter's hand cuts lines in vigorous strokes, or that it was *informed by a graphic energy correlative to the organic force of nature.* And none could say of the scribe something similar, that the pen of the scribe is driven across the page and around its orthographies and grammars by a singular force. This cannot be how words are produced, since they are overly governed even when rebelling, or if not rebelling, even when words are written in despair, or with words thrown down as litter is dropped without laying claim to any kind of territory or future, those words are never spontaneous or natural, each word is not its own original, nor are these words carriers of inspiration. Not even the monk at Lindisfarne could claim it. That last letter, the letter b, last written before the monk was killed by some accounts, was only aborted and never driven by the force of vision, and to the extent it was corrupted at its edges, or perhaps smudged, or grotesquely extended by the killing blow, it ceased to be a letter. The only inspired act, the only gesture that might be correlative to the organic force of nature, was the raising and the falling of the axe.

None could say of the woodcut, as they have claimed of the ink or paint-drawn image, that the chisel of the cutter *nowhere flags in the energy of its creative function,* or that *every mark records the force of the original inspired gesture.* A writer who studies the woodcut might well arrive at the same conclusion, and say, *none should say this of us either.* Inscribed words, or marks formed by numerous cuts, grow as much from a confusion of positions, or at least carry no single origin. If each cut made by the woodcutter is inspired but overshadowed, if each word placement carries its own unique force but relies upon its context, the assemblage of cuts and words remains a medley of intentions, even a mockery of origins. Perhaps the worst thing about writing, then, is that moment when the author sits back from their work and finds the effect somehow affirming, of themselves, of what they intended, of what they were or would hope to be.

Yet few have truly written as the cutter cuts. Writing remains driven by the pen, or the image of the pen, or by the burin and its portraits. Few have written as the cutter cuts since the removal of text by deletion—the writer's equivalent to the woodcut—still leaves traces of the mark, and the mark retains the image of the pen. Writers engrave, or mark, they do not cut however much an author may say so and might lament it. In most cases the activity of deletion is for the purposes of contraction—the remaining words narrow into the space left vacant. Or if the space is left as evidence, it is blank, featureless. Either way, the deletion of words cannot produce infinitesimal recesses, or voids of inexpressible detail.

§

See the land as the woodcutter might view the woodblock, is how a particular group related me their theology. Or perhaps this was how I divined it from their words and way of looking. They saw the intentions of the God-hand on the world only at its highest points, along the ridges they at times visited, and on the mountains they could never surmount, knowing all else was the voided space needed for the isolation of sole peaks and for the delineation of extended altitudes from those neighbouring. They saw the lines and flecks, the hatchings, and scores, as they imprinted on the sky. So not then from above as if looking down, nor from below imagining up, and not then at all with the literal gazes of land and water creatures possessed with eyes and transported to do some super-terranean looking. These high points were understood as liberated from the sunken land and noticed in their flat geomorphic characteristics. They had the capacity to swell and taper, taken as expressions of tension and relaxation in the God-hand's work. And so too was felt their own absence from this design, this knowledge that the God-hand was unfeeling and not even disinterested before the details of the valleys and gorges through which their lives were stretched. This lack of regard freed them below to live without regard of themselves.

They only climbed the ridge to remember constraint, and fully know again, were they subjects, should they have been below of the God-hand, how all their goods and all their evils would amass before and behind them, and they would submit to their own servitude. On the ridge they built cave-recesses and covered retreats, but these were only with the view to existing alone while up there and taking shelter, and had been abandoned, eventually, for the structure they subsequently built, buttressed outward, an extended lament, also an extended manifestation of the fact of being seen, an outgrowing and cantilevered complaint that reached up and atop and over the watershed. It was built for its internal, ridge-superseding possibility, a series of inner passages that had become their ridge-walking diversion. Within the artifices of that erupted architecture all manner of experience was pursued—including all deviances and every imaginable act of libertinage from every known angle—resourced of the kind of diligence and focus usually absent from their lives.

For me it was an interruption. Crossing inside during my travel on the ridge, my eventual exit was facilitated only by the exhaustion of its internal possibilities, each and all assigned their rooms, every room with at least two doors so that no single room was left by the same entrance. The God-hand was felt in all of them, pushing its occupants from different directions but just as definitely whichever way they contacted, and there was no passing through a room without submitting to its distinct motions and cries. Exit was contingent upon experience. And so it was all variations of human contact were felt in all sequences and types of pressure and touch and secretion, but with the exception of those rooms that left permanent marks upon the bodies of their occupants, that maimed or injured, or in some cases killed—again with infinitesimal variation—these rooms having along their length a glass corridor so that visitors could pass through in safety and without committal, should they will it that way.

I spent several months merely in those chambers devoted to the variations of human breath. Here I began to appreciate the broader meaning of the labyrinth on the ridge. I knew of its basic mechanics—the necessity of passing through its rooms—and hoped still for a final exit and return. But I had no understanding of its function at first, of what this building, which cantilevered out either side and grew from those outgrowths into expanding towers and side-towers, had to do with the migration of peoples from the valleys below. Most rooms were devoted to a kind of breath that could not be enticed into words, such as room after room reserved to breathing differently on the ankle of another, or those for the exploration of the coughing breath, or the breath sounds like laughter could emit. Eventually the breath

experience migrated upwards and finally to the head—the
back of the head was subjected to interminable variations of
breathing and for which we were shaved to better feel it. When
it came to the breath of mouths before mouths, I discovered
some kind of rudimentary conversation would be possible. This
was done by breathing word-like gusts in the face of the woman
valley dweller, and then in the face of the man, and eventually
the child, as the rooms cycled too between different types of
breather, and the different shapes and emissions of the lung.
The words had to be breathy words—which means a variation
of breezes—for the valley dwellers were otherwise mute, indeed
not a resonant word had been spoken since the last word I
heard outside on the ridge and before entering. This word, or
last string of words, had been prompted as I commented on the
rough edges of the structure, viewed from its exterior, and this
comment I made brought a response from somebody nearby
also walking in its direction, another person, like myself, who
was about to enter and would spend months, perhaps years,
inside. This person, hardly worth describing otherwise, I saw
transfixed much later in one of the killing rooms, submitting
to its specific angle on the question of infliction—in this case
impalement—as I myself spectated from the glass corridor. The
reply he gave before we entered the labyrinth was curiously
vacant at its beginning. And here was the trace of their valley
in the mechanism of speech. But that reply reached some kind
of resolution by its end and seemed to mark a transition in
language from profligate speech issuing from an indeterminate
nothing, or a nonlocalizable something, through to reasoned,
which is to say rationed speech, and finally to the annulment
of the word, and then to the first silence of the first chamber

which would perpetuate throughout no matter how painful
the tortures of the room. There were cries, of course, but no
exclamations or commentary.

§

During my transit I met with other ridge walkers too and the
turrets they built and visited. These were arranged at intervals.
Each bears the sign of the God-hand in relief upon its bricks.
The hand resembles a flat thrust gesture, fingers held close
and straight, thumb fingerward too, and of the sort a midwife
readies before getting to with the investigating. I have seen it
done. When faced with the turret there is no way of proceeding
except through, given the sides of the ridge are invariably sheer
about the base and the turret is generally overhanging, and so
the going in must be done like the hand described, the head of
the one entering leaning in at the entrance and the eyes tight
with it, or they pop, so they say, at the transition point. Once
admitted, the ridge walker will adjust to the atmospherics and
produce his or her life to the expectations of the interior—
always narrow, profusely so—or so I gathered from the first
turret, and then, upon moving to the next turret, must regather
and extrude something different, and so it goes until a ridge
walker has lived several lives or at least several different ideas
of what it means to live and lie among others. There are ways
off the ridge, downward paths and iron stairways, and I assume
those coming from the valley only endure as many lives or
ideas of living as can be lived, before walking off the edge and
returning, that is to say, who most of them must turn back
before reaching the supple state of somebody who has lived
through too many turrets to count, and might be described as

123

plastic, or at least open to different versions of the same thing, the body thing which first entered the first turret, and exited the last, with some variations naturally.

§

Reaching the ridge they achieve the mark of the God-hand, so they say, or so I have come to understand by applying one metaphysical framework after the next. All frameworks will do to explain their behaviour but the one I arrived at did best. This drew analogy to the activity of the woodblock cutter, or the down-driving God-hand to them, the divine meaning-giver who left the ridge standing alone—after all of the carving—as the only mark worth attending and worth imprinting to the heavens. But with the heavens moving over, the imprint tends to drift.

Strewn across the ridge, they too reached the status of that mark, and the taller they stood, the less the ridge imprinted on the sky in relation to their dotted supersedence. At times standing was done in a uniform line some distance long—they stood five paces apart—and the ridge mark, their watershed, was overdone. This overdoing was achieved so long as they remained with their heads clear above it.

Each head was marked with ink, the sign of the imprint, even though ink was too literal for doing what was otherwise imagined. They knelt and daubed it over. Raising their arms then after, the imprint was next of tiny hands, again blackened

with ink, and not the dark crown of the head which makes a
better and more definite dot. Either way, from a distance, the
effect was similar, they felt.

. . . .

The raising of inked hands was just another way of mirroring
the God-hand, mirroring it by reply, by a sort of imitation,
a miniature doubling, and so thinking it by doing that done
away with, which it never was. This was a self-regarding rite, so
I thought, that was stood for so long as they could manage. In
the line of a whip, theirs was a temporary humanism.

A heretical sect once dwelled here too, digging pits in the ridge
to reduce its continuity of definition, and there are stretches
of the ridge that are considerably decayed by their pitted and
pockmarked past. This sect taught that the ridge walker is wrong
in thinking to grow the ridge upwards by their being there.
That would be a confused reading of the activity of woodblock
cutting, and if they are to rise above the valleys at all and seek
the definition of the ridge, it should be to repeat the activity of
the God-hand driving downward, to observe the logic of the
cut-making by continuing the work of carving, and by digging
spread the voids that were the valleys below by voiding the
ridge at intervals. This would serve to further absent the lower
realm from the upper one.

unununununununununununununun

But when they stood up after digging, simply to stop the back from seizing up, it looked a bit different.

u-u-u-u-u-u-u-u-u-u-u-u-u-u

To another sect, none should have been on the ridge in the first place. Leaving the valleys was an insult to the intentions of the hand—it was the mark of hubris.

§

Arriving at the ridge from the valleys below, the unrelatable part of the world was retained in the activity of the ridge walkers, carried onto the ridge by those who suddenly appeared monstrous in relation to the law of the ridge, which was already word, or letter-arrangement. They were pushed into the pits dug along the way, to pits supposedly dug by another people since those I came upon did not arrive from the valley with digging implements. Their now isolated kin—all in some form, form-defying creatures—were spectated over from the rim as I knew from being inspected myself, first by their heads, and then their shoulders, and finally down to the approaching shins. This was how they came to look at us.

I found myself among one small, wildered group of those like me freshly cast as abominations—all of them fellow valley dwellers not long before—and decided that I, for my merit, was there due to my plasticity, and can thereby boast to have lived among deviants who make a mockery of reason just as they defy nature.

The truth about these deviants, that they did not exist as such in the valleys, is a kind of lie, but that lie only materialises on the ridge.

It is one of the great injustices of this ridge to see how those who cast judgement from the spirit of their own self-told acceptability did not become recognisably monstrous on return to the valley.

§

The valley from the perspective of the woodcut is, when printed, a white space of absence, or a near white void, depending on the paper used for the printing, and so, not at all the dark abyss of the typical void, or the void as it is usually figured. This void is voided by the disappearance of matter, whereas the white void is voided in the reflection by matter of too much rather than too little colour. It resembles those valleys hid under their morning mist leaving the hilltops striating, only, a mist has far too much detail for the analogy to hold, and not enough fibre. White voids still come in different forms, though. For otherwise the same might be said of the engraving—its voids are also white. These white regions correspond to the polished segments of metal, near featureless plains that neither retain nor transfer ink. The void they engender is more literal, it is the void of the burnished flat, of the unscored copperplate, whereas the void of the woodcut is a kind of deceit. The detail is all there, it is merely the fact of its not being transferred, or of how the inking and ink transfer does and does not happen. Which means that reproduction, and the production of white space, is the fabricant of the lie.

§

Walking left from the room in which all books on the forepassed topic of hermaphrodism are to be found, I reached the front gate. It is difficult to walk with any kind of precision within the wall, and for this reason I had not seen the entrance for several weeks.

Arriving at the doors, he left the wall for a short space. The air outside was tasteless. This was nothing, but that nothing of a sort he could deal with. And yet, the light of the flat against which he was grown unaccustomed could not be taken for more than a moment.

Once returned I did not come across the room devoted to hermaphrodism as soon as wished for. Or had I wished it, getting there could not have been immediate. Either way, my return was not for some time, maybe days. Eventually, when back, the place was much smaller than I recalled, perhaps approaching the outer limits of what might be known as a cubicle. Its stock was similarly reduced. Indeed, the room had shrunk to perfectly fit its diminished holdings. This may have occurred with some of the larger rooms, only these were made smaller by a less evident retraction, being larger to start with, and did not strike me like this one did, as immediately different.

I estimated the regression to be that of a century, perhaps more. Taking a book down from its shelf, it was still possible to read—

By the decision of the Paris parliament in the year 1603, a hermaphrodite who had chosen the male sex dominant in him

*was convicted for having used his other sex and was condemned
to be hanged and burned.*

But I could no longer access statements from a subsequent
century after things had changed a bit on the question of
hermaphrodism, and in which a doctor is called instead to
examine a defendant, determine the dominant sex, and so
decide which clothes were appropriate and how they were to
live. This would determine also how they would die—in the
appropriate clothes—but no longer of what, or when, and so it
was often to be a natural death, shod right. It would seem that
from the vantage of my cell, these doctors and their decrees
had not yet been born.

Measuring the regression was no easy business. I wandered from
case to case and could not gather with the precision I wished
for, that I felt I deserved, how far had been travelled in time. The
record these books held—their record of my transit—was set
to confusion, or was not readily available, or legible at a glance.
The fact of a book being printed in a particular year did not
mean my being there post-dated the book. Books printed later,
that is to say, after my existence, but which referred to earlier
events, were still in evidence, whilst their temporal equivalents,
which referred exclusively to contemporary events, were gone.

The quote which runs, *By the decision of the Paris parliament,*
actually derives from a book printed in the future, in the mid-
eighteenth century. This book I now took from the shelf was
largely intact, but thinner. The explanation of their thinning
is simple enough. Those books which referred to past events
and contemporary ones in the same volume, were missing the

latter pages, yet were bound as if those missing pages had never been printed, the gaps only evident from the errant pagination.

Of these thinner books, one or two spanned a mere few pages, the only sections in which past events were related, and even on those pages much of the ink was gone from where the author lapsed back into their present, not able to sustain narrated history, or narrated recollection, for more than a sentence or two.

During this visit, the holdings declared the wall in which he walked to be standing astride the latter half of the seventeenth century.

In a subsequent visit the room was a recess, then it was a shelf. At last, a few slots in a wall in which he found the *Book of Marvels* of Phlegon of Tralles, untranslated, in the original Greek. This placed him sometime in the region of the second century.

§

Returning to the site where I had once read, or thought I read, *By the decision of the Paris parliament*—it was apparent the room was shrunken, and most probably too the innards of the wall, leaving me here with Phlegon's *Book of Marvels* in which there would be no mention of Paris, indeed no other manuscript in the entire holdings of the wall did mention the city, since Paris as it would come to be, could not yet exist. The complete absence of Paris as I have known it from the purview of all known and all forgotten books—including books rumoured to have been written but which in actual fact never were—testified to the century I since entered. It was the second or third. Phlegon's

Book of Marvels was nonetheless translated, and this translation was into modern English. The book was also bound in the modern way.

§

Phlegon records seven instances of hermaphrodism. In the first, a man named Teiresias visits his foot on two copulating serpents, or, in a different version, hits out with a stick. By some accounts, the female serpent is struck or squashed, in others it is the male. In any case, Teiresias went from being a man to being a woman and had intercourse with a man in the latter form. Apollo advises striking the serpents a second time, and Teiresias becomes a man again. He is subsequently consulted by the gods as to which, man or woman, derives the greatest pleasure from sex, gives the wrong answer to the one god and has his eyes gouged out, gives the correct answer—the same answer—to the other god and has his life extended and is given the gift of prophecy. Teiresias lives not one, but seven lives, all of them eyeless, unable to find another serpent, forced to talk as a man and be heard as a man, and so condemned to being a man for much longer than most men must endure, a man who has seen men from the perspective of a woman.

It seems to be insufficiently appreciated, writes one scholar, *that the basic events of the Teiresias story match those of an international folktale* in which a man becomes a woman, lays with a man for seven years, has seven children by him, and then, as the seven years are up, turns back from woman to man, returns home, and greets his wife not minutes after he left.

131

In the third instance, a young maiden in Antioch is struck by excruciating pain on the morning of her wedding. Treated for three days for stomach gripes and cholic, on the fourth her discomforts are stronger, and with much additional wailing the young maiden extrudes a complete set of male genitals.

In the fourth case of hermaphrodism, something similar happens to a maiden named Philotis, this time upon her betrothal. In the fifth the man is made man in order to become a gardener—a rare example that does not involve wedding-avoidance. Of the sixth instance Phlegon writes, *I myself have seen this person.* In the seventh case both sexes are noted as present from birth. The oracles are consulted and recommend copious sacrifices, which is to say, the delivery of money and meat, for the child is judged a prodigy, a sign of some future calamity. This calamity must occur, and can only be put off and placed beyond the lifetime of those first affected by submission to oracular rite. Given that each transformation with the exception of the seventh is viewed as an improvement—for the man emerges from the woman— each remains a marvel rather than a crime against nature or law. There are several other texts in which similar examples will be found—mainly women becoming men by the irruption of a tumour, and so on, with one man even joining the cavalry and fighting under Alexander. In all cases, the appearance of the male organs is noted, and this by their natural extrusion or surgical extraction following pains. Which accords with Galen's treatise *On the Usefulness of the Parts of the Body,* in which the male and female organs are said to be morphologically identical, they are merely reversed. The female anatomy is not really worthy of inspection for this reason if a man already has all the materials of knowledge at hand and need only reach down for it. In any case, each instance of hermaphrodism is recorded in passing—given it is not experienced as a fundamental disturbance—with Phlegon himself swiftly moving to a description of various giant bones, in the section entitled *Finds of Giant Bones*, an account that may also be read in the other *Book of Marvels*, an identical book, which is lodged in a separate room in the wall, the room devoted to giant bones. This room would later include a copy of *The City of God* in which Augustine writes—*the large size of the primitive human body is often proved to the incredulous by the exposure of sepulchres, either through the wear of time or the violence of torrents or some accident, and in which bones of incredible size have been found or have rolled out.* In a later century this room would grow and eventually split between the rooms of the megafauna and those of the dinosaurs, and then those devoted to larger hominids, initially assembled together, and then separated out into the various sub-groups, including a chamber for homo erectus—with antechambers in which subspecies were arranged, the eponymous *homo erectus erectus*—known from a single specimen dug up with the assistance of convict labourers, incorporating a tooth, a skullcap and a thigh bone, and once described as resembling a giant gibbon—and *homo erectus soloensis*—known from a mere 14 skullcaps—and then another much larger chamber for the much made of neanderthal, and so on, and naturally not a single chamber devoted to homo sapiens—all chambers had that characteristic—although there were specific rooms devoted to those sapiens suffering from gigantism, hyperostosis, macrocephaly, osteochondroma, and various other afflictions, and those judged to be not actually hominid, a fluctuating group. For Phlegon, who focuses on the bigger bones, the evidence was arranged to different ends, which is to say, as confirmation that mortals were taller in earlier times and bore closer resemblance to the gods. Herodotus recounts the discovery of a coffin containing a skeleton seven cubits in length, and a footmark the Scythians liked to point the gaze of visitors at that was two cubits long and was imprinted somehow in rock. *In Dalmatia*, writes Phlegon, *in the so-called Cave of Artemis one can see many bodies whose rib-bones exceed seven cubits.* In the time of Tiberius Nero there was an earthquake that razed many cities and opened cracks in the ground. From the sides of these rifts emerged numerous, large skeletons. A tooth of one was extracted and measured to more than a foot. Augustine reports something similar—*I myself, along with some others, saw on the shore at Utica a man's molar tooth of such a size, that if it were cut down into teeth such as we have, a hundred, I fancy, could have been made out of it.*

Phlegon goes on with his list, begging indulgence to the credulous—*One should not disbelieve in these bones either, considering that in the beginning when nature was in her prime she reared everything near to the gods, but just as time is running down, so also the sizes of creatures have been shrinking.* The senescence Phlegon observes is cosmic. The energy of the universe is dissipating, and to this diminishment the semen of men falls victim.

The younger Pliny, writes Augustine, *maintains that the older the world becomes, the smaller will be the bodies of men.* And notes too that *Homer in his poems often lamented the same decline.* This idea is one that Pliny *does not laugh at as a poetical figment*—and Augustine does not laugh at it either—*but in his character of a recorder of natural wonders accepts as historically true.*

Phlegon tells of another coffin, this time a hundred cubits long and containing a withered body not much less in proportion on which is written, *I, Makroseiris, am buried on a small isle / After living a life of five thousand years.* Phlegon does not comment on the marvel of self-burial and self-inscription. Or, to look at the problem with a gesture of respect, Phlegon does not question the veracity of first-person address, and thereby identify the first lie of narration with this "I" which is presumed. Ancient epitaphs are often addressed in that way, and the first-person novel of a subsequent age might be originated here where the "I" who speaks is at best a revenant, but more usually quite simply and permanently dead. The paper, or vellum, or papyrus, has more life in it than the "I" which is printed there. These materials have at least once lived.

There is only so much that can be said of bones found, measured, and re-interred, Phlegon suggests. Or thrown in the sea, as did once happen—an act that only a barbarian people could be guilty of. Phlegon moves on again swiftly, now to monstrous births—

A highly respected maidservant belonging to the wife of Raecius Taurus, a man of praetorian rank, brought forth a monkey. Or the woman of Tridentum who brought forth snakes coiled into a ball. Or the birth of a child by the male slave of a soldier. Or the ghost which ate a new-born hermaphrodite leaving only the head which, having no other parts of the body to concern itself with, began to talk at length about various matters of not inconsiderable importance.

And deaths—the person who was born, grew to maturity, was wed, had children, became old, and died, all in the space of seven years.

Pliny the Elder tells of a Greek woman, by the name of Alcippe, who gave birth to an elephant.

§

Makroseiris was a Greek-Egyptian compound. A withered giant found resting on a nameless island lays the Greek adjective *makros* into the side of the Egyptian god of the deceased. The remains of a word hybrid, which might be translated as Long-Osiris.

As Plutarch recorded shortly before Phlegon's own time, the myth of Osiris has the god reign a mere 28 years, or live a mere 28 years, at the end of which Osiris is tricked into his coffin. As the story goes, Typhon arrives at a feast with a magnificently adorned chest. He will present it to the person who most perfectly matches its length. Osiris lays down in the spirit of the joke and does perfectly fit, whereupon Typhon and his fellow intriguers slam shut the lid, seal the coffin with lead and nails, and throw it in a river that delivers the chest through the Tanitic Mouth to the sea, *whereupon even to this day the Egyptians name this mouth the hateful and the execrable,* writes Plutarch.

Isis, sister of Osiris, will find the coffin, but does not bury it. Typhon reclaims the box and sends the bones to all corners of Egypt to be separately interred.

The skeleton, *Makroseiris*, may still be these exact remains, but for this to be true, followers of the cult of Isis-Osiris will have to gather the bones and reinter them. These bones might also need to grow a stretch and do so where they were buried in the fertile Egyptian soil. Unless Plutarch forgot to mention the fact of their extraordinary length.

§

In the chamber that is devoted to pseudo-archaeology, one author writes that she has traced the burial to a small island less than a mile off Cape Zoster, and about thirteen miles south of Piraeus. Its entirety contains Neogene sediments, so it stands to reason that diggers would turn up the great bones of the mammals of that period.

§

It is recorded that Typhon was born from a blow dealt to his mother's side. And that he leapt forth and so issued not needing to learn how to leap. Almost needless to mention, if a new-born knows how to leap, he can surely before that walk, and if a new-born can already walk, that child must be able to sit, and if a new-born can already sit, he can hold his head, and if before all of that he can strike his way out of the womb, he is hardly born and hardly child. So much for Typhon.

Isis, the sister of Osiris, was born the next day, writes Plutarch, and she came to the world *in the regions that are ever moist,* whatever that means. Osiris preceded them both. It is also written that Isis and Osiris *were enamoured of each other and consorted together in the darkness of the womb.* How Typhon occupied himself, meanwhile thereabouts, is not mentioned. They consorted together, or at least Isis consorted with Osiris once again after Osiris died, for which Isis had a member especially made to do the consorting with. Upright in all other respects too, Osiris was the first lawgiver. One of his first acts was to *deliver the Egyptians from their destitute and brutish manner of living,* it is written. He later travelled the remainder of the earth and civilized it too, which would mean that anyone subsequently found, as they have been, in a less than civilized state, can only have themselves to blame.

Osiris himself was also undone, it is true, and it was his own doing to let it happen so, making Osiris the first carrier of civilization, and its first self-inflicted disaster.

§

Isis found her brother's coffin on the advice of some children. They guide her to the mouth where it was let to the sea. The effect of this story has been of such lasting influence that many adults have looked twice at children, wondering if all the little noises they make, and all the senseless talk and chatter, might not be mere childish undertakings after all. And so, other little children in subsequent ages have been listened to, as if they, too, possessed the power of prophecy or at least of decent perception. Those most deserving of an ear will be found playing in holy places, *crying out whatever chances come into their minds,* writes Plutarch. Fortunately for the children concerned most adults tire quickly in their company.

Isis did not find the coffin precisely where the children indicated, and not even in the region suggested by them.

One part of Osiris could not be reclaimed. The god's pisser was tossed in the river and subsequently eaten by the lepidotus—an extinct genus of Mesozoic fish—as well as the sea bream and the pike. When his sister had a replica made to take its place, the phallus was consecrated. The manner of its construction is not reported. Fleshy, wooden, of bone or stone, none would subsequently know. When faced by the above fish, Egyptians abstain to this day, writes Plutarch.

Some say the phallus was tumescent, others that the words of the ceremony were swollen, since surely only words could swell once Osiris was dead, and Isis was glad.

It is said the distribution of bones was not the doing of Typhon, who did not send them across Egypt after all. Rather, it was the sister's ploy, and the bones were not real and could well have been of the Neogene. False Osiris bones were set down to confuse Typhon in his attempts to reclaim and finally obliterate the brother. And big bones were chosen. The sending of false parts would also ensure that all major cities had a so-called tomb and would be encouraged to worship her brother in perpetuity. Which meant there was no proper tomb among them and there were no true remains to gather, but only pseudo-remains and pseudo-tombs—although not pseudo-worshipers and pseudo-sacrifices. If these pseudo-bones were subsequently raided and their parts reassembled, we must admit that the so-called giant, *Makroseiris*, may well have been a consequence of the aboriginal deception.

§

The full and complete verse of Empedocles may be found in various rooms, for it is the tendency of older texts to have broad relevance to a number of different concerns. And so, in the same room that I read Phlegon's monstrous births, I came across an argument made by Empedocles, the so-called pre-Socratic, about the creation and destruction of doomed creatures.

The distinction between a monstrous creature and an ordinary one is simply a question of survival. All short-lived creatures were abominations, whereas those which have offspring, and which survive and reproduce were not, could not be considered abominable, and so a human child with four heads—as Phlegon reports—was a sign of the anger of the gods, whereas satyrs and centaurs were to be accepted. Or to state the problem with greater precision, the gods favour creatures which are like their parents, a law most children would prefer to disbelieve until they have their own.

When Eros was ascendent in the cosmic cycle, and Eris, or strife, was *on the back foot*—an expression that as yet made no sense, there was no back foot—the separate appendages of humans and animals came into existence—feet, heads, arms, eyes, claws, and so on—and were driven to merge by the force of Eros. These newly created appendages became connected in all manner of arrangements, each assemblage a chance event, with eyes quite possibly and more than occasionally taking it all in from the end of a finger, or the pit of a midriff. Arrangements that did not function well together, such as the head of a man and the sphincter of an ox, perished, even if Empedocles' daughter, on hearing her father's analogy, suggested this was a good and workable system—an intervention he did not take in good humour.

She had just finished scribing the words—*Where many heads grew up without necks, and arms were wandering about naked, bereft of shoulders, and eyes roamed about alone with no foreheads.* This was the fourth iteration of the passage and is the version known to history. Her father also dictated—*Where many arms wandered past heads, just as alone, but motionless, and eyes were set to roll.* And other similar versions that were discarded and only ever known between the two of them. She would often tell Empedocles that if he came up with another iteration of a passage already written, she would send him to the moon. And he would joke it would suit him just fine, and he would live well enough on a diet of lunar dew.

In one of those peculiar accidents of history that brook no explanation, the second century satirist, Lucian of Samosata, fires Empedocles to the moon from Mount Etna. This some six hundred years later, and has him survive by feeding that way, on dew, doing a good deal of high thinking upon it.

Not finding his daughter at all funny in regard of the sphincter comment—since this joke of hers took aim at his philosophy—Empedocles left the house for several days and set his mind against the etesian winds. These were about to visit their usual violence upon the crops, except Empedocles made use of his own violent temper by ordering asses be flayed and bags be made of their skin. These he stretched out on the headlands and hills to catch the wind, which they did. The crops were flattened as usual, but Empedocles had it recorded by another how it was a round success and the inhabitants now knew him by a fond nickname, the wind-stayer, which they did not, of course, because this was not his achievement, and they were a bit low on asses as a result.

§

Centuries later, so much detritus had accumulated the Romans could not help but trample most of it underfoot. In some rare cases an item was extracted from the earth and sent to one of the various temples. Here it would serve the so-called tourist industry—to adopt a term from a subsequent age. These objects gained value for being consecrated there. Books were deposited, strange animals too, and these temples became museums of a sort. Even a clod of earth might do if it smelled of human flesh—it was claimed that before the temple at Panopeus lay some pieces of the very clay from which Prometheus made the first men. At Olympia, the horn of the goat that suckled Zeus. At Carthage, the skins of three hairy women caught on the west coast of Africa, later thought to be gorillas. At Rome, the skins of several gorgons encountered and killed by soldiers during the Jugurthine War, but later, much later, thought to be a strange breed of sheep. At Erythrae, the horns of the Indian ants. At Sparta, the egg that Leda laid, later, again much later, thought to be that of an ostrich. And at Coptos, and somehow at Memphis too, the very hair that Isis tore out in agony over Osiris's death. The bones of the beast sent to ravage Andromeda were paraded in Rome by Scaurus—these were longer than the ribs of an elephant. And, centuries later, but still well within the period of antiquity, the bones of a whale large enough to hold fifty bears were exhibited by Severus in the amphitheatre. Gluttons were also paraded. A chronicler reports that at the time of Nero there was a glutton named Arpocras who was seen eating a boiled pig, and following that did eat a live hen with all of its feathers, and then a hundred eggs to prepare the way for a hundred pine kernels, several hobnails, broken glass, the twigs of a broom, four tablecloths, and a sucking pig, and then, as an insult to the dietary needs of the pig, a bundle of hay. Arpocras managed all this and still seemed hungry. Some said that Nero wanted to give the glutton live men to chomp on and thereby see how well they would go down too.

During the two most productive centuries of a much, much later time, where scholars of a sort prospered in the already then ailing humanities, scholars who preoccupied themselves with such minutiae as these, it was debated whether Arpocras the Glutton was in actuality a crocodile. Others suggest he must have been an Egyptian and have proved at length these were the feats of a man, and that this kind of eating could only conform to the imaginary of men not crocodiles. That Nero had a pet crocodile is not disputed, although it may have been a hippo. He liked to pat the creature on its head with its keeper perched on the snout and would tell it things the creature could never imagine and would never do.

This can much of it be picked and parsed out from a volume of *Roman Life and Manners Under the Early Empire*, by Ludwig Friedländer. The version in the wall contains a preface by the author, although there are other details which indicate this book was not a future book read in the past. The hairy women later interpreted to be gorillas, the gorgons later decided to be sheep, and the egg of Leda subsequently considered to be that of an ostrich, suggested it so. These intrusions would have been redacted if I was to read the book long before the book itself had been published. And so, it is reasonable to think I might have been reading it around 1913, or shortly after.

§

The distinguished philologist, Ludwig Friedländer, had a brother. This brother was no less distinguished in his day but was subsequently forgotten in a more absolute sense than Ludwig was himself forgotten, as most scholars are indeed eventually overridden, even the best of them. The brother wrote books of similar seriousness and renown, except, every few pages the brother would introduce a falsehood, a false claim alongside a correct one, and with it caused many subsequent scholars to waste hours seeking out the source of this or that novel intrigue, as yet unknown to antiquarians. The story about Nero and his crocodile-patting habit is one such example. It was followed by hours of futile searching, for which the brother was subsequently found out as a fraud, and had his books so deliberately, so systematically ignored by his fellow antiquarians, that they were eventually lost and the man himself was too.

The older Pliny claims that the hippopotamus is itself a notorious glutton—a word that still only applies to men—and relieves the pressure of its belly by scraping along its undercarriage from which wounds the animal bleeds, and by which bleeding it partly deflates.

Gluttons were still marvelled at long into the second millennium, with Browne recounting a story first told by The Most Reverend Olaus Magnus over a century before of a *devouring ravenous quadruped, frequent in Lithuania & Moscovie,* known as the *Gulo* or wolverine. The creature was said to fill itself until it could eat no more, and then compress itself between two trees specially chosen for their close standing. By this doing it *squeezeth out through the guts what it hath devoured, and then filleth itself agayne* as before. None of which could be accepted if not for the observation of that famous professor of Leyden who dissected such a beast and found it had no division to its gut, no folds, nor complications, corners or cæcum to speak of, but that it was one rotund ingesting organ, and so everything it held could be squeezed forth as one, and as easily as it was ingested.

The idea of eating a human is often introduced to the animal by man, either directly—here have some of this, dog—or simply for being so often in the way of the animal that flesh-eaters feel impelled to do something about it. Even elephants lose it, on occasion.

§

Valentinian had a bear named Innocence and another named Goldflake. These he maintained on a diet of criminals.

§

Severus also had a pet glutton, as did Aurelian. Each was assassinated—the emperor, not the glutton—which was less unusual than the gluttony.

§

It was not out of character, notes Friedländer, for Roman tourists to depart from the various temples displaying marvels, such as the stone that Cronos was duped to swallow in place of Zeus—several temples boasted one of these—or the skin and tusks of the Calydonian boar, rotted and devoid of bristles, or the hair of Medusa. For indeed, they had spectated on these objects to the point of boredom, and took themselves off to go seek marvels further afield. Some would make for the pyramids. The Egyptian tombs were then covered from apex to base by a smooth surface up which locals strode at speed to impress visitors with their surefootedness. The writer and philosopher Abd al-Latif observed around the year 1200 that these surfaces were covered in hieroglyphs and that these signs would fill more than ten thousand leaves. Which means if they were transposed, more than ten thousand leaves would be required to reprint them. The analogy is symptomatic, reducing a monument for a moment to its writing, a situation the ancient Egyptians facilitated more definitely than any other ancient culture with their mark-making incontinences. This reduction of monument to print, or the thought of how many leaves it would occupy if it were to be printed, is a striking reduction even if, or precisely because the writing was still, at this date, completely indecipherable. It might be said, though Friedländer does not himself say so, that the idea of transposing the pyramid across ten thousand leaves actually razes the brute spectacle, the great edifice of the monument, by analogising it as printed material, and that this shows how the written word had by the time of Abd al-Latif evidently come to surpass all other rivals, all other traces of human intention, all other extensions of human artifice and mark-making activity, and so, rendered archaic already then the heavy stone and earth structures of the near past, as well as the further past, as they are superseded by the heights achieved in language, and that language even then rendered archaic or downgraded in advance those monuments that would follow, which had not yet been constructed—the cities, cathedrals, and sculptures of the future—which are all of them already superseded by writing even before they are quarried, cut, and lumped together, and from which supposition it is not at all nonsensical to say indeed, that the most perfect architectures would be those that could only ever exist in writing. Such is the conceit of the written form. The depletion of this outer layer of the pyramid—or the destruction of this text—was accelerated in the fourteenth century, writes Friedländer, and by 1395 a French pilgrim noted the erosion was near complete, at least for the Great Pyramid and its smaller cousin. The second pyramid fared better. It was mostly intact until as late as 1638. Among the lost inscriptions were those cut by Greek and Roman tourists, mainly their names, but occasionally memorials to companions who no longer trod with them.

—I saw the pyramids without you, my sweetest brother, and for you I shed as many tears as I could here, and in memory of our grief I engrave this lament—

Some of these Greek and Latin messages were recorded by pilgrims headed for the Holy Land, being more relatable than the hieroglyphs themselves which remained illegible until 1822.

Friedländer's brother claimed that the pilgrims and even the women among them liked to climb to the apex in groups of four, and that they would urinate from it and down each side and see whose piss rivulet reached furthest toward the bottom before drying out. This was one of the brother's more obvious fabrications. It is impossible to reproduce in any case, and test, as the pyramids are not only well-guarded, but have become stepped.

Thomas Browne is more respectable in the manner of desecration when he writes—*But to subsist in bones, and be but Pyramidally extant, is a fallacy in duration.* Yet Browne does not pay due attention to mummification in his HYDRIOTAPHIA, URNE BURIALL, OR, *Discourse of the Sepulchrall Urnes lately found in* NORFOLK, and did not sufficiently delineate his vanities, so that the vanity of tomb burial, and the vanity of the pyre, is accompanied by a third vanity, that of the organ-deprived body lodged in pots with the exception of the hardened and withered skin. At most Browne notes of how Egyptian ingenuity was *more unsatisfied* than other burial rites, but what of its specific vanity, there is no detail. Browne is more focused on dissolution, on how the mummies of his century are put on show in various countries and given whatever names are fancied for them. Consumed by avarice, the mummy has become merchandise, writes Browne, and the Pharoah *is sold for balsams.* When it comes to mummification, the fallacy of duration still applies just as it applies to the monument, since duration, or so-called preservation, guarantees at best the production of a sign which reads, MY PEOPLE HAVE FORGOTTEN ME, MY PEOPLE ARE DEAD. And even this sign itself barely deserves a passing glance to those, writes Browne, *whose generations are ordained in this setting part of time,* and *eye the remaining particle of futurity* with disturbed ease, knowing that duration, which hastens in the atomic age, and still again in the age of hunger and heat and thirst and raids and migrations, will at last *maketh Pyramids pillars of snow, and all that's past a moment.*

§

In reply to a letter seeking his opinion regarding the nature and antiquity of the various burial mounds or barrows to be found about the land, Browne raises them above pyramids in their endurance. *Obelisks have their term,* writes Browne, *and Pyramids will tumble, but these mountainous Monuments may stand, and are like to have the same period with the Earth.* But for Bateman's incontinent digging, of course. Further evidence, as if it were needed, that Browne himself did not feel the impulse before *diverse heaps of Earth* to turn them over and draw their insides out.

§

The existence of Friedländer's brother is only known through a single and somewhat errant copy of his translation of *A Collection of Marvellous Researches* by the ancient Greek compiler, Antigonus, which contains 177 fragments, rather than the usual 173 known to have survived. This translation is attributed to *the brother of Ludwig Friedländer.* Three of the additional fragments are obvious fabrications, since the brother makes his presence known directly—there is a clear autobiographical imprint. The fourth will only be discovered by direct comparison. In the first category, Antigonus' observation that the guts of sheep differ in their sound-making capacity, so that the guts of rams are soundless, whereas those of ewes are melodious, is followed by a comparison between the brothers made in similar terms. *I for my part have a most melodious gut, whereas my brother knows only how to rumble.* A similar analogy is offered in relation to the account Antigonus gives of a Sicilian thorn which, if it injures the foot of a deer, will render the creature's bones useless for the making of flutes. The brother of Ludwig Friedländer writes that his bones, like his gut, are able to sing, whereas Ludwig's bones, and his guts, know no melody.

§

Antigonus claims what when copper ore is smelted in Cyprus, a creature slightly larger than a fly is produced of it, and that

150

the same happens in the furnaces of Carystus. He also claims starfish are so hot they catch their prey by touch, causing them to boil. And that every creature bitten by a rabid dog becomes rabid, except man, who is born demented.

§

There are places in Persia, writes Antigonus, where pregnant mice have been dissected and found to contain embryos already themselves pregnant.

§

Another book of marvels, *On Wondrous Things Heard,* was first attributed to Aristotle and only subsequently assigned to an unknown figure known as pseudo-Aristotle. It might date from the third century before centuries began again. Having not been in the wall during this century, I cannot verify that. There are clear overlaps with Antigonus, yet both authors may have been drawing from another common source, since lost.

I continue to read all of these documents in modern English, typically holding them in those many centuries before that language was organised and policed to become what it is, the language I know and treat with. There are creatures described there, by pseudo-Aristotle, that seem to me rather like those which still appear in the upper shoulders and passes after the ridgeline ends. Each encounter is essentially beyond proper speech and could be better left that way—for their part the nomads do not comment on what they come across—and I would have left it alone myself but for the happenstance of finding creatures in pseudo-Aristotle which do not exactly match, but nonetheless stir my memory about a bit, and so render something of what might be seen.

And so it is, there is a mountain in Paeonia on which climbs a beast with a hide great enough to cover eight couches when skinned, that flees even when incapacitated, and protects itself by voiding excrement, which it also kicks, voiding and kicking over a distance of forty feet. The stuff will scorch the hairs off the back of a dog. When protecting their young the creatures gather in circles and project in all directions.

There is a bear with breath so foetid it will decompose a dog and phlegm that will choke and blind a man—when blown on the face.

And a species of cliff-goat that does not drink like other quadrupeds but opens its mouth to the wind.

And a leopard that seeks out human excrement, which is hung from trees to tire the creature out.

And birds that retire into holes in the winter and do not void. These may be plucked and pulled over and down upon a small spit and will not feel it.

And a whirlpool into which animals may be fed, be seen to drown, and come to life again.

And a crevice between rocks into which is drawn such a strong wind that a pipkin, when lodged there, will bring its contents to the boil.

And a tree that sprouts branches that wither up and disappear at night.

And some mines in Macedonia that grow silver from their spoil heaps, and a type of bronze in Cyprus which, when cut in little pieces and sown, sprouts and produces more of the same.

And mice which eat iron, and other mice that live in mines and reveal their diet of gold when cut open. They say too that there are parts of the world where mining does not happen and digging is futile. All pits and excavations fill as soon as they are made.

And that among the Ligurians there are slingshots so accomplished they will have a discussion amongst themselves before a flock of birds concerning who will take which one there flying, so assured are they that all will be downed.

And there is a river the Ligurians know of which flows so high that a Ligurian stood at one bank cannot see a Ligurian stood on the other.

And a scrape of land not more than twenty stades across in which a variety of barley grows that will kill a horse, and not even pigs or dogs will touch the excrement of men who have taken a barley meal.

And a stone called *wise* by deliberate contradiction, for whomever picks it up goes mad and kills one of their relations. And a stone called *dagger* which has the same effect. And a stone like ivy which changes colour four times a day and may only be seen by girls who have not yet reached the age of discretion.

And a patch of land not larger than a threshing floor where animals perish immediately with the exception of the cantharus beetle. These little creatures arrive and scuttle round until they die of starvation.

§

Antigonus, Phlegon, and the other compilers of strange phenomena in antiquity, *shewed no interest in theory*, their style was simple, and they only adopted the guise of Alexandrian scholarship and not its spirit. Each marvel is presented without explanation or attempt to relate it to anything else. These were indeed some of the lowest forms of classical writing preserved, designed merely to titillate, never to edify. They hold the least value to historians, and none at all to serious thinkers.

—that was the argument of Ludwig Friedländer against the paradoxographers, a judgement levelled too against his brother.

If strange things are to be, not so much believed, but encountered, they must be separated from their originating contexts and become their own norms.

—this is the only surviving sentence written by the brother of Ludwig Friedländer, and it works well enough as a reply.

§

Modern scholars have largely treated the paradoxographers—Antigonus, Apollonius, Phlegon, Florentinus, Vaticanus, and so on—to the twin privileges of omission and neglect. Yet in the early twentieth century a study was written in which their work is described as *a parasitic growth on the tree of historic and natural-scientific literature.* In the mid-twentieth century there followed another treatment in which the genre is described as *arid,* and *a degeneration of the interest in the marvellous,* and as *a purely collectionistic mania drained of religious concern or ethnographic curiosity,* and finally, *a banalization of taste that became a mass phenomenon.* In the late years of that century, a more sympathetic reader describes this tradition of writing as *recreational reading,* or *entertaining reading with a flavour of learning,* or *a kind of popular literature,* or as a kind of *writing that aims to be broadly accessible by making minimal demands on its readers.* Sympathetic readers can often be more catastrophically dismissive than hostile ones.

§

It is typical of the paradoxographers that they would only conceptualise a marvel as a thing that occurs in the recent past, and not in mythological, or cosmic time. A marvel is always a near-contemporary thing estranged from more reasonable assumptions by some adjustment or other to its expected behaviour or to the understood properties of a thing. The materials that make up a marvel are ordinary, or commonplace—a threshing floor, a goat, a pipkin—which means all strange occurrences carry a degree of ordinary perception within them. They are only strange because of the residual knowledge, the dominant effect, of the ordinary against which they are compared. These ordinary things are perturbed, admittedly, but to the paradoxographer there is no possibility of reorganising perception without them.

And so, the paradoxographers are judged badly by the system they cannot disturb, as parasitic, or degenerate, or as being purely collectionistic. Aristotle must become pseudo-Aristotle, the art of assemblage becomes pseudo-scholarship, and knowledge is held to be trivialised.

The paradoxographers only appear in the guise of their rejection, as already subsumed within a symbolic order that has been hardened off by serious thinking. They remain no good to think with. And if they have described some of the creatures beyond the ridge, these creatures will be among the most ordinary, the least surprising, and so the most easily rendered of those I met with. It may be necessary to travel to a time before perception was organised by academians and their kind. A time before efforts were first made to regulate learning and insist that statements must stand before inspection. If that were possible.

Only the Cynics maintained some measure of resistance against the new learning, and so it goes that when Crates came upon an ill-educated boy, he hit the boy's teacher. Crates strikes at the very person who should be able to save the boy from his lack of education. And with it draws attention to the first paradox of learning, a paradox that the well-meaning and virtuous cannot solve, *who will teach the teacher.* The answer is of course already given. It begins with the stick, or the cudgel.

But this is the limit of Cynic intervention. It may well be that Empedocles or what remains of Empedocles is of more use in describing the upper regions, those beyond the ridge where the nomads pass no comment on what they see. That is to say, it may be necessary to pass a few centuries before the first paradoxographer.

Of the nature of God, Empedocles writes—*he has no human head fitted to a body, nor do two shoots branch out from the trunk, nor has he feet, nor swift legs, nor hairy parts.*

Ordinary things, heads, bodies, shoots, a trunk, feet, swift legs, and hairy parts, these are negated by Empedocles to no purpose at all, except in saying, *not that.*

Of the nature of the heart, and so too a man's intelligence, Empedocles once said—*The heart lies in seas of blood which darts in opposite directions, and there most of all intelligence centres… for blood about the heart is intelligence in the case of men.*

If Empedocles is right, by man's judgement man must have little or no intelligence at all in the bloodless sense of the word. Empedocles manages, then, to both tell at man's expense, and insist in that same gesture how intelligence will be conceptualised herein on, as essentially divergent if not also given to clot.

And of the rest—*Many creatures arose with double faces.*

§

The nomads pass comment on everything they see, said I, and each line they speak is taken from Empedocles.

—*thrice ten thousand seasons shall he wander apart from the blessed,* say they, *being born meantime in all sorts of mortal forms, changing one bitter path of life for another.*

157

These mortal forms are hardly described, merely indicated, and their various appendages are not counted. They are entirely unlike the Zoroastrian three-legged ass with its six eyes and nine mouths—three of which open in the face, three in the forehead, and three in the creature's loins. Or the Christian beast with seven heads, ten horns, and ten crowns each carrying a blasphemous name.

Each number for the organised religions is a code, applicable to a universe that has emerged from chaos and can be reckoned, if only obliquely, by religious cyphers and deferrals. Even 666 provides a kind of security, the satisfactions of the code-giver and the code-reader. Empedocles envisages no such place. The only settlement Empedocles imagines is when all things amalgamate to become a supremely all-incorporating cosmic sphere across which surfaces no counting may occur. There is nothing to tally up and no mouth to tally with.

—Then neither is the bright orb of the sun greeted, nor yet either the shaggy might of earth or sea; thus, then, in the firm vessel of harmony is fixed God, a sphere, round, rejoicing in complete solitude—

§

The mouth is produced of strife and Eros and follows the obliteration of the perfect sphere and the death of the fixed God.

The fixed God, the God beyond the reach of nature, the God as perfect sphere, the God with no exterior, and so no dominion. That God killed the god that killed all pagan gods and did so despite their comparative vitality. All gods, including the God that declared itself the only God, as others declared for it, can be seen to be done away with by Empedocles.

The fixed God could have no mouth, this god, the sphere, would have to disintegrate long before a mouth could come into existence to issue its divine command.

The mouth can only open and begin to omit sound once the cycle has begun and things like mouths can be made. Strife punctures the mute, unknowable sphere that Empedocles divines, and causes its countless dispersals to begin against the draw of amalgamating bodies, all of them fugitives even when amassed.

Some of these bodies have nonetheless become rooted, or so the civilized believe. But if a settlement has been reached against the implosions of love and the divestments of strife, if a minor and derivative but habitable sphere has perhaps been created from of the cosmic dust upon which self-possessed creatures regard their lives with some measure of satisfaction, if a second orb, less beautiful than the first, and yet divine in its way has grown to *the shaggy might* of enduring sea and earth and has become its own apparent absolute, studded now with wandering creatures, and hills, and forests, and things that fly and fall with predictable ease, the nomads do not know it.

Along another path I hear the words—*For mighty Air pursues him Seaward, and Sea spews him forth on the threshold of Earth, and Earth casts him into the rays of the unwearying Sun, and Sun into the eddies of Air; one receives him from the other, and all hate him. One of these now am I too, a fugitive from the gods and a wanderer, at the mercy of raging Strife.*

The nomads say too how they *wept and shrieked on beholding the unwonted land where are Murder and Wrath, and other species of Fates, and wasting diseases, and putrefaction and fluxes.* Or this was how I remember them, their mouths opening so rarely that lines of film contracted those lips as they talked.

§

It is surely wrong to place the words of Empedocles in the mouths of the nomad, but less wrong than using the words of those who came after and spoke once verse was abandoned.

Aristotle claimed *it would be absurd if anyone, saying that the sea is the sweat of the earth, thought he was saying anything distinct and clear*—and then points to Empedocles for saying it. Such a statement, writes Aristotle, *might perhaps be sufficient for the purposes of poetry, but not at all for the knowledge of nature.*

The same would later be said of Aristotle's cosmology—it merely happened to last a while longer before it was refuted and came to appear fundamentally risible.

Empedocles did at least open with the line—*scant means of acquiring knowledge are scattered among the members of the body; and many are the evils that break in to blunt the edge of studious thought.*

And yet, Empedocles would still write closer to the gods.

It would be better to say that when the nomad speaks the sound is that of a trailing wind, or a river, or a hailstorm, or an avalanche—that is to say, the product of multiple collisions, or occurrences, or what the electronic age would perfect as static, or would be sung, by approximation, as a death growl.

§

On a trip of a kind that we are swiftly abandoning for the railroad, I sat with him, and suffered his company and conversation without let-up, writes Friedländer of his brother. He took advantage of our entrapment by horse and carriage and told me of a period when the intellect did not yet exist. When it did eventually come into existence, so he said, the intellect swiftly forgot that kind of thinking which subsumes the thinker within the thing that is thought. This was the condition of its emergence, he declared. The intellect was firstly and forever after productive of itself.

As our carriage continued through the forest and took us further to those gradual erosions of self that travelling people of this pace and duration will know only too well, he switched topic and related his latest attempt to translate Empedocles into modern German.

There was a time when it was not at all strange or presumptive for Empedocles to write as if he were not a mortal man, I was told. Nobody would have thought it odd. And with this remark he returned from the second topic, Empedocles, to the first, the intellect, implying, so I thought, that Empedocles was not an intellectual and that Empedocles recalls an existence before the intellectual came into being.

§

In his introduction to *The Dissertations of Maximus Tyrius,* the translator commends the 1804 edition to the English reader.

These dissertations, once offered by the Greek rhetorician and now rendered again for an intelligent public, are only a partial remedy, he admits, to the mighty evil of this degenerate age, which considers nothing worthy of attention that *does not pamper the appetite or fill the purse.* Scepticism abounds, and nothing is believed that cannot be held or directly seen.

In the first volume, Maximus mentions the semi-legendary poet Aristeas, *in whose wisdom all men at first disbelieved because he could not adduce any one as his preceptor in it.*

—which was already out of time when Maximus first wrote it. And this stands to reason, since it was written in the second century or thereabouts, eight hundred years, or so, after the poet. It had by now long made sense to ask, but who will teach the teacher.

Aristeas could not adduce anyone as his preceptor because the poet was his own tradition. He was the origin of what he might teach. He never answered nor need he answer the question, *but who will teach the teacher,* or *but who told you that.* In an inspired age, the question makes no sense and only a fool would ask it.

The poet claims to have done a good bit of travelling by wafting his soul from his body and journeying by way of it across the air. Aristeas saw across every island, river, and mountain, and from there to the edges of the world. He surveyed all political manners and all conceptions of law and came to understand them. So too did he see *the mutations of the air, the flux and reflux of the sea, and the gates of rivers.*

All of which Maximus explains by introducing a second anachronism, the anachronism of his Platonism. If the soul had no eyes to look with, then how did it see—well, simply, by *converting herself to intellect.*

As does happen, there is a different version of the trip in which Aristeas travels in a divine stupor, or trancelike wandering state. This must have been a travel-facilitating derangement, or so it has been said, for the poet gets so far north as he can by way of it, and to where the ground is frozen iron hard, and gleans all he knows of the furthest regions, those beyond there, from the tellings of a people who stew and eat their dead mixed together with a bit of mutton.

§

The consumption of dead relatives is not unusual in pan-historical terms, and Aristeas was not the last to observe it. A thirteenth century traveller laments the very same thing, or what he describes as *a strange or rather a miserable kinde of custome. For when anie mans father deceaseth, he assembleth all his kindred, and they eate him.* And so it is that these people, judged abominable and odious to all other nations, make *no other sepulchre for them, then their owne bowels.*

Another observer might consider the parent-eating habit remarkably efficient. And did not Thomas Browne himself draw attention to the dangers of monumentalising the dead, of erecting excessively ornate tombs which act as a distraction, a dangerous diversion, from the coming oblivion.

—*the long habit of living indisposeth us for dying,* wrote Browne, thinking only of his own kind.

And when Browne wrote with the distance of a sage—*Our Fathers finde their graves in our short memories, and sadly tell us how we may be buried in our Survivors*—he did not realise that the very same wisdom was already enacted by the cannibals who might have said—*Our Fathers find their graves in our stomachs, and tell us how we may be digested in turn and done through by those who follow.*

§

Some say the soul of Aristeas left his mouth in the form of a raven. This meant much flapping was entailed during the course of his travel to the far north.

Inelegant, then, when compared to someone like Abaris the Sky-traveller who rode upon an arrow given him by Apollo, and so traversed the seas, the rivers, and the mountains of the earth by way of it, and escaped a plague too, and more, on his pointed stick. But the arrow is referred to by Porphyry as a *so-called arrow*, suggesting that Abaris flew by transmigration too, and that his soul may have been seen wafting just as that of Aristeas did waft from the mouth.

This, by the way, was the same Porphyry who wrote the widely censored and so lost *Against the Christians,* in which it is claimed that the miracles performed by Jesus were *nothing special* alongside those performed by the ancient Greeks.

§

The far north was not the only destination of the soul of Aristeas. Some years would pass during which his body lay prone, and the soul appeared in various places announcing a coming plague, or an earthquake, or drought, or flood. And then departing.

§

When Maximus describes the return of the soul to the body of Aristeas, he says that the soul treated the body it came back to *like an instrument.*

§

When Apollonius describes the return of Aristeas, the soul comes to the body *as into a sheath,* or into a *vagina* as differently translated, to *arouse it.*

§

A small correction to the Empedoclean account is needful, said he. The cosmic cycle will return to produce again the cosmic sphere, or *total mind*, the *encircling solitude* of the omnipotent all. This when Eros triumphs and dissimilar things are pulled inward to admixture, and so lose their distinctiveness and certainly their consciousness. The sphere is a fixed god without subjects and yet a god in the purest sense—a god that returns only on the condition of the extinction of all beings, and births them once again only on the occasion of its own cosmic death.

AND MOREOVER. Strife, or wrath as it is otherwise known, does not only drive things apart, but can attract things too, but only if they are similar—the rest it chases to oblivion as usual.

A great heap of earth may amass from similar particles by the action of strife. And when untouched by Eros, will remain lifeless. Presumably eyeballs would come to lie in heaps too, or coalesce in bunches, and this again by the action of strife, or so it would be if only they did not also contain a little fire. The eyeball is actually a combination of two elements, according to Empedocles, or at least according to the daughter, and the best composition or recipe of the eye *is when it is a compound of both fire and water in equal proportions.* Those eyes with an excess of fire see less well in the daytime, Empedocles continues, and better at night.

—something Pausanias knew as well as anyone, for Empedocles is believed to have desired the man, as they say, and came for him most urgently after dark. I see clearest at the end of the day, he would tell Pausanias.

By some accounts it was the latter's daughter who scribed Empedocles' verse by dictation, and not the daughter of

Empedocles whom now, so the accounting goes, had none of his own.

Pausanias, to whom the whole lot of the Empedoclean bequeathment is addressed, was also promised the gift of raising the dead, and so too his other children who died in childbirth or of an early age. Which makes greater sense if we consider that Empedocles made a habit of employing them.

—*And do thou hear me, Pausanias, son of wise Anchites*, it begins.

§

A good stretch of time before Empedocles, Anaximander offers his own assessment of the origins of the world and all that exists within it. All things emerge from *the boundless*, a spatially limitless, and ageless material that is so uniform and so limitless Anaximander need not say, nor can he say any more about it beyond naming the thing, or not-thing—and perhaps even this naming is too much. The philosopher hardly even explains what comes next, apart from suggesting—so the records say—that *something productive of hot and cold* is merely *separated off* from the boundless.

As a distinguished commentator once observed, this act of creation *looks like little more than an abstraction of mythical masturbatory genesis by a single male god.* A point the scholar nails by then observing—*especially since the Greek word for separate off can also mean secrete.*

167

Empedocles, to his merit, appears to recognise the mistake of even speaking anything he has thought. This must include the repeated mistake of all who have ever spoken, or written, ever since, including the scholar who subsequently wrote about *mythical masturbatory genesis.* Each word is already itself inadequate—the words of mortals cannot comprehend the gods or god-like things, and if the world separated off from an effective nothingness, which is at the same time, an all-too-muchness, and did so in a wondrous discharge, the concept of *masturbatory genesis* and the image it conjures could never capture it.

The same goes for so-called birth, a preferred metaphor among men. For when they say *born* this word has the advantage of referring to what they know to happen but cannot experience and need not fear again for themselves.

Empedocles, once more, is circumspect. *For there is no way for what-is-not to be born,* writes he. *And for what-is to perish is impossible and inconceivable.* These concepts are inadequate descriptors. Nor can there be in the totality anything empty or overfull, for there *is only a mixing and then a separating of what was mixed.* Yet by *mortal men these processes are named beginnings,* and so on.

§

The enduring fallacies of the word and its world meant that by the time of Thomas Browne it was still necessary to remark— *there is nothing strictly immortall, but immortality,* which must surely mean that the word *immortal* becomes a victim of its vapidity. Every thing is in flux, and no thing stabilises from instability, nor achieves the status of permanence outside of God's realm. When we look for incorruption in the heavens, even the stars must divulge themselves as alterable in their parts, and *perspectives begin to tell tales.* Or when we look to the sun, the spots that wander around it state that our sun, too, is within the reach of adjustment. But these words Browne uses have become even more futile in their expression. They do not call words, all words, into question as Empedocles once did.

Browne has taken up residence in language. Empedocles still had mutton in his teeth.

§

Meaning to pass the time on their journey, Friedländer casually asked his brother how he knew when a new intellectual project had begun, and how he felt when one ended. It is unlikely that Friedländer cared for the reply, though he did record it. His brother replied, so Friedländer reports, that he, the brother, often had an idea, a vague intuition of what he would like to next pursue, but that a new project would never really start until he opened a fresh notebook and began writing, and even that moment was not a beginning yet. Once the words had gathered some kind of generative momentum, once the project had started to produce itself and take a form that felt worth inhabiting, then he knew, after the fact, that it had begun. Or, to put it differently, his brother continued, so reports Friedländer, *I can only begin a project by writing something that I know cannot survive.* I begin by producing words that will, by tearing off a page, or through gradual attrition by transcribing and rewording, slowly migrate to something else. There are no real beginnings happening here, said he as the coach continued to jostle them about inside. Writing seems to me more heavily weighted towards expulsion, sometimes of entire passages, but mostly of things that were only ever half-formed. Most ideas are terminated, axed, or fizzle out before they have the opportunity to become something. This is largely what I do, said the brother.

Friedländer and the brother had each once read that line from Empedocles who claims, when men talk of things being born or of beginnings, and when men talk of things ending or dying— *Their language follows their rules.* To which Empedocles then adds the crucial supplementary clause—*and I too assent to convention.* Which meant that even he, Empedocles, lowered himself to words like birth, or dying, which had no application in his cosmology.

Friedländer took this to mean that there is nothing outside intelligibility—the stuff of his mind—and so he need not take strange notions such as Empedocles' cosmic sphere seriously, or Anaximander's elemental boundlessness. Friedländer was typical of his age in that respect, remaining untroubled by all he touched, or read.

The brother understood it all differently, and the very same *I* which said, *I too assent to convention,* suggested to him the necessity of elemental suspicion before words, before which he, too, would submit out of necessity, and would even use the authorial *I,* this elemental writerly deceit, just as Empedocles submitted once long before to another, earlier language, in order to make himself understood. In this respect, the brother took the perspective of the sphere, or the boundless, insofar as that perspective may be taken.

§

The great procrastinators, Friedländer later wrote, were the greatest writers. This, according to my brother, or the logic of my brother, who killed off more words than he produced and considered this elemental writing.

And the best of all writers remain silent, his brother also said, which Friedländer described as just another example of his brother's vapid wisdom.

§

During the carriage journey, Friedländer's brother had much else to say, or so Friedländer claims.

—What defines the first seekers after knowledge, and sets them against the poets, writes Aristotle, said he, is that they recognised only material principles and laws as the prime movers, and relied no more, or not so much, on mythological explanation. In claiming this, Aristotle did not realise how the first seekers, Thales, Anaximander, Empedocles, and so on, were driven beyond themselves by a god-like impulse, and that he too carried it. Yet Aristotle's was a more fussy, lower-level incarnation of the godly impulse, the brother continued. *Aristotle is the stationary organiser, the paperclip and pen lid holder among gods,* my brother said holding a pen lid to illustrate, *and all philosophers have followed in that profession.* They hold their pen lids, shuffle their ink pots, and do their best Godly work with them. He held his against the carriage door window, so placing it before the lines of the trees that were blackened flat.

§

It was also rumoured that the brother had a considerable collection of blotting paper in his possession, and that he gathered these papers by stealing into the offices and studies of anyone he could gain access to, and that he had somehow managed to avail himself of the blotting papers of some of the most revered and foremost philosophers of his age, and that he wished to make a library of them.

§

The suggestion that the earth is barrel-shaped was rivalled by another ancient idea, that it was flat, or largely so, and that the sun and the moon circumnavigate along a strip around its perimeter. Their rising and setting would be accountable by some particularly high mountains at the edges behind which the heavenly bodies disappear. These mountains should not have been unlike those I visited, and down from which I myself came on leaving the nomads for the flat—the last of these nomads were lice-eaters.

Other fabled mountain chains also resembled this region I was coming to abandon, such as the high places inhabited by goat-footed men, and the far-off uplands beyond which men were said to sleep for six months of the year. Or die for six months, it depends on the translation. I may well have glimpsed them in their holes.

Seeing the plains ahead of me now, I saw they too resembled the Scythian lands described by Hippocrates, or the edges of those lands that were themselves said to be on the approach of the edges of the world—*a part of the world which Nature has written off.* I have found this description authentic in its detail, insofar as Hippocrates describes a region which *holds the icy womb where the north wind is conceived.* Yet Hippocrates says too that the region is *buried in thick murk,* and this is plainly a fabrication. As is the claim that *a thick fog envelops by day the plains upon which the Scythians live.* These very same plains before me now, those that would have the Scythians live there one day and would outlast their extinction and loss to caricature, were, as I could see, more likely to be afflicted by a featureless sky.

§

According to Asiatic lore there is only a single mountain, or world-mountain, at the edges of the earth. It holds up the sky by some accounts. Or carries at its tip the north star. By other reckonings, when looking up we stare across the inside of the mountain, at least by night, which would make the stars and the galaxies mineral deposits.

§

The transmission, if not the invention of folklore may simply be a question of confused prepositions, it has been said. Where *above* means not *to the north of,* but actually, *on the far side of.* Or *below* means not *to the south of,* but in fact, *on the near side of.* That is to say, things that were considered far off, were actually nearby, and nothing was originally distant or out of bounds.

In a rare book entitled *Gigantic Walls and Open Spaces* it is claimed that what a wall gains in length it loses in definition, since it can grow and begin to bulge over a very long distance without notice, and can narrow out by a similar degree, again without notice, so that the wall will become as thick as an engorged snake—fatted as if it had eaten a city—or as thin as a thread, without anyone thinking to comment. The only condition is that the wall is extraordinarily long, so that those walking its length will forget its width by the extreme gradualism of its adjustment. The author takes this idea to its limit and suggests, if a wall is sufficiently long, all territories either side, such as they exist, will merely be within the areas of its thinning. This wall would not be fatted *as if* it had eaten a city, but would have actually done so, whereas in the regions of its thinning, those left outside of it—and this must include the city where I grew up—are in the region of a kind of retreat, and there is no other land to speak of. Open spaces have the quality of tidal lands which come into existence upon the basin of a distended ocean. But whereas tidal land is nourished by the daily return of the sea, the open spaces left by the wall in its thinning phase are abandoned to the sun, causing the land to rot and desiccate.

§

Within the wall there is a chamber which is, not so much a holder of books, but a consequence of various arguments made within them against the intellect. Those books containing these arguments will be found there, but can only be touched, and have been allowed to decay and moulder and nurture the spores that were lodged and dormant within their pages. The growing out of books makes them more fragrant and multiplies their surfaces. The room is entirely soundless, and completely dark, for if sight and hearing are the theoretical senses, they must be denied in favour of taste, smell, and touch, which they over-rule by a decisive not tasting, not smelling, and shrinking before touch that the intellect developed as its second nature, as its prime mode of abnegation. These senses are too material, or too lodged within what material reality extrudes for taste to inspire a thought that is not directly tied to the wetness of the tongue, or for smell to conjure an idea that does not reek or has no perfume, and for touch to generate a concept that cannot be grasped or directly suffered by the skin. When isolated from the dominion of seeing and listening, from showing and making heard, it will be found that these books are nonetheless prolific in their effects. From their wetness, and their stench, they reconfigure the intellect, connecting it to a molecular, or even atomic array of forces and imaginaries—for want of a better word—that have more variety and mystery, than any book will manage.

These are some of the arguments made in a rare book entitled *Gigantic Walls and Open Spaces.* I may well have encountered that book in the room to which it refers, though by definition I would never know. It was surely read elsewhere.

The intellect, it goes on, is presumed by intellectual beings to exist at a higher plane, *where the so-called intellectual creates his double, his shadow, where he feels more himself by placing himself above and beyond himself.*

Two days initially spent watching them in their holes, from the first irregular breath indicating the beginning of the waking process, to the first sleeper no longer sleeping but sitting upright.

It should have been minutes not days before I left the sleepers behind me, walking myself between their hollows and paying them no further attention as I continued to the flat. These hollows, I saw, lay not to any particular line of the compass but followed, in their rectangular inclination, the shifting contours of the slope against which the holes were dug. I should have left them there, I first said, and said again, laid out and under, but to an open sky. Their limbs in a state of ordinary paralysis, or near-total paralysis, as ordained by some hinder part of the brain. It prevents the actualisation of dreams into which they emerged for one last, extended interval, after six months of deep retreat. This came after the usual, but for them vastly extended subconscious stupor of nothing much thought, not even the nothing much thought of an unreality, but the nothing much happening of not being neither one thing or another. This was the long silence that was broken in their waking, with the arrival of that last but hyperactive stage of sleeping, which is the time of dreaming.

Usually a mere sliver in time, a few minutes, lasted hours, days, for these sleepers. It might be said of them that their reverie, the half-conscious and amorphic visions of that period of return, must surely last decades in turn, due to the drawn-out transition of their waking. Just as ordinary waking may fill a minute with an elaborate drama of several hours or multiple episodes, their waking dream during the course of this slow return from six months of slumber, brought those lying there to live much of a lifetime, or fragments of several lifetimes in that state of partial consciousness, and so it was these sleepers felt as though they, or something of them, did all but die upon the realisation of their departure from it, their having left a vision, this by now well-stocked unreality which had grown to be preferred to the waking state. Their extended transition to wakefulness was felt to have been lived so long it could only be lost, or reduced, as a dream identified as such, and thereby annulled, by way of the annihilation of a long sensation, as the expurgation of a world, as the cry of many billions of beings expiring at once, which is what it was to them. This waking they went through was not what waking usually is to the typical sleeper, which is to say, a moment of return that is a moment of correction, often relief, a defogging, the usual and mundane daily righting and refiguring, over which passage the person who wakes both acknowledges and accepts it was not real, that it did not happen, and so need not be regretted as the annihilation of a world might be, even a world in miniature. Which is how it clearly was to them when they opened their eyes, and gazed at their stasis, and saw the poverty of their reality in the hollows they occupied, and promptly returned from the abject torture of this pale waking state of a hill slope to the hope for another lifetime beyond the earth and slate of the shallow pits within which they slept and their bodies gradually decayed.

§

A celestial goat, or perhaps it was a stag, is rumoured in the deepest mines of China, as it once was. When those who dug their tunnels downward came close, the thing would beg of them to be taken to the surface. All attempts were made to hinder its ascent, sealing off otherwise rich seams, closing galleries that were not yet exhausted, trapping and sacrificing men if needed to block the creature and muffle its pleas, for when it did manage the surface, as did sometimes happen, it liquified on arrival. The land above was infected. Over it was spread a thick, tar-like pestilence.

§

It will have been observed by some scholar, somewhere, that the goat-footed men were actually mere goats, and that the men who slept six months of the year were hibernating bears. The modern tendency to explain the inexplicable will always render it plain. Yet bears do not hibernate in large numbers together, nor do they lay themselves down in open pits. This behaviour is characteristically human.

§

Pliny the Elder claims that the Greeks all agree on one thing— the art of painting originates in lines traced round the human shadow.

For the Romans, art originated somewhat differently, and more directly from round their own bodies and the bodies of others, of which they left copious, on the battlefield especially.

§

Pliny died by asphyxiation amid falling pumice and cinders from Mount Vesuvius, and was only retrieved from the field in which he fled, and fell and died, many days later, leaving a Pliny-shaped imprint in the debris. Pliny went across that field, so his nephew reports, with a pillow tied to his head by a napkin.

Others claimed Pliny was nowhere near the volcano and died of a regular heart attack, and that there was no void in the ash and pumice of a Pliny-shaped kind, and so, no lasting imprint, nor artistic statement. He was, by all accounts, a corpulent man.

§

SUPPOSE A BOOK into which errors are allowed if not welcomed, redoubling the work of hearsay, poor transcription, rumour, and fabrication. These were as productive of ancient texts as the truths they sometimes retain. Falsity, or at least a degree of fakery, would generate another way of thinking, and another way of supposing, in a book like this.

§

The ability to fabricate where truth is expected—the sign of an undomesticated mind.

§

A book which tells lies alongside truths, and then forgets which were which. Or reads a revered text one day and tells it another without the text to hand for the retelling. Allow recollection to stutter and fill in false detail.

§

And from it all find solace that some things are still malleable, they can be taken by the hand, or the finger, and moulded or prodded into contusion, when most things have been taken out of the grasp of the prodding or creating hand, and have been determined elsewhere and by a time in which the art of creation, if it ever was, has been lost, and all things are undergoing continual making and re-making by reflex and incorporeal impulse.

§

It makes no sense to adopt the compiler's art from within the wall where all books are extant. The compiler observes at least two impulses, the need to preserve books that may become lost, and the need to gather books in a shortened form so that these summaries can travel more easily than the library from which it culls and cumulates its text. Each impulse has no place in the wall, nor can the compiler exist outside the wall, at least not in those times when the wall became fatted to encompass all things.

§

Libraries can no longer burn; they are already in the air. The perfect facsimile of all surviving books is easy and instantaneous. The activity of hording has been mechanised, and the extraction of text has become a matter of automated reading. There is nothing left for admirers of truth or accuracy but submission to the absolute, unalterable veracity of the text. We resign ourselves to becoming the footnotes, say they, and are transformed into little textual engines themselves.

When the wall became fatted, the work of the scribe, an entire profession, was at last relinquished. Books will not be saved by laborious recopying. No scholar will carefully transcribe words before the paper, papyrus, or stone on which they are printed, is lost. A compiler occupies this relinquished space, and recalls an earlier time when truth was a casualty of transcription and errors were commonplace if not an art in themselves. A compiler returns something to reading and to writing of the mechanics of picking up, turning over, and distorting, if not catastrophically over-looking books which were left to rot, or would be remembered only in fragments.

Within the wall and its chambers there would naturally be more than one volume of Browne's PSEUDODOXIA EPIDEMICA *or, enquiries into very many received tenents, and commonly presumed truths.* Also known as the book of VULGAR ERRORS.

Browne's work on error and superstition has application in most fields. The problem of error and error expurgation, and of superstition and its overcoming, is so common between them that the *Pseudodoxia* will be found, in part at least, in every subsequent chamber of the wall and subfield of knowledge that grew—as all did—from hostility to so-called vulgar untruths, careless mistakes, wanton errors, or deliberate falsehoods, or whatever name it was given, and was produced as a field, or as a specialism, from an impulse to correct, and self-correct, and observe against those who pretended at knowledge but had no place among the learned. The *Pseudodoxia* was an earlier and gentler manifest of the love of rectitude that subsequently produced those pinched and restricted creatures later centuries would call the good and the clever, the correct and the proper, all those, in short, who would be called and would call to heel in the name of truth or rectitude. Against which Browne remains somewhat distinct from all ensuing pedants and plain-makers, even if he trails a similar odour.

—Browne's corrective, his encyclopaedia of falsehoods, retains some credulity for the fancies it reveals. His was the more tender pen that strikes off and to unreality each superstition or mistaken belief it treats.

—Browne's pen seeks not to address the people—*the multitude; that numerous piece of monstrosity*—by which Browne means all other people of the other sort. And in consequence, Browne's pen has no widespread educational intent. This is to say, Browne's work is not propelled by a corrective or instructive didacticism that takes aim at the enhancement of all minds and their thinking spaces, and so, will not call its carping at the idiocies of others a kindness, or a virtue, or a calling. We have not *addressed our Pen and Stile unto the people*, writes Browne, since *Books do not redress* them. If the space of learning is to be tidied out here, and herein, and by way of the *Pseudodoxia*, this will not be extended to the tidying of all minds in the shadow form, the pared back and impoverished form, which owes its existence to the grand abstract form of the educated person.

Widely imitated in the barking conceit of the schoolteacher, the grand abstraction reappears in the very idea of themselves they travel with, of how, without schoolteachers all would be lost.

§

THE FIRST AND FATHER-CAUSE OF HUMAN ERROR—this should surprise no man—it is the common infirmity of the human condition, writes Browne. It yields to hunger, to enticement, and will neglect the hardships that truth demands as its condition and effect. Human error of this sort derives from the aboriginal mistake of Adam in trusting Eve.

Of the second cause of error, the people bear responsibility. This is the error which becomes widespread and gathers its own populace, so that one might accurately say, the people as they aggregate become Error in its very self. All men may be infirm, but the people assent to falsity with a kind of willingness, a tongue-led surety, which suggests they surely have especial taste for it, says Browne. These people are to be lamented, *they live and die in their absurdities, passing their days in perverted apprehensions, and conceptions of the World, derogatory unto God, and the wisdom of the Creation.* Their delusions are nonetheless interesting. Preferring parables to prepositions, and finding proverbs more powerful than demonstrations, their approach to language is literal, they have no taste for the second or the third intention of a text, and God himself is reduced to *manual expressions.*

§

183

Of the word *exantlation*, not much can be said. Its lifetime is unusually short, lasting from 1646, or thereabouts, which is when Browne first uses it, to 1704, when the word appears again in Swift's *Tale of a Tub,* referring in each case to the *drawing up* of wisdom, from a well, or from an incision. This oddly short-lived word may quite possibly derive from a common source— the verbal habits of a doctor known to both men, the doctor Browne knew, who was also the doctor Swift came to know, each meeting that doctor when visiting London. Swift does remark in a letter since found, how his London doctor had a passion for words, and for this word in particular, and would say when venting an abscess, *this here abscess will be the site of my finest exantlation to date.* It is no overstep to presume Browne knew the very same doctor and heard the word in a similar context. Both Browne and Swift were influenced in this particular word usage by the very same man and his inappropriate anatomical verbosity. Only, for this to fit, the doctor would have been very young when Browne first visited before or around 1646, and the same doctor would have been still living and working when Swift—who was not quite yet born when the word first appears in the *Pseudodoxia*—arrived in his care towards the end of that century. Naturally, it is neater to believe the word originates with Browne and not the doctor, and that the doctor acquired the word from Browne as the latter neared the end of his life and transmitted it to Swift not so long after. This will surely become the agreed-upon explanation. Browne the originator, his doctor the conduit.

§

When Browne sought the advice of fellow practitioners as his own body began to give in, he omitted mention of having himself used leeches on others to *bleed at the hæmorroid veines,* but did more than once recall, so as to not cause suspicion, how *Syrup of Tabacco is good, and men I observe confesse much benefit by it.* And went on to note how *a quarter of a spoonfull will help to expectorate and cleare the lungs; a spoonful and halfe cause a vomit.* He then remembered he had already had a couple that morning.

§

Browne laments the credulous air of the Greeks, *which swarmed so with Fables, and from such slender grounds, took hints for fictions, poysoning the World ever after,* even as he remains beholden himself to the mind they conjured. Their legacy is full of wisdom still, but merely requires a trifle bit of pruning. It should be easy enough for the diligent-minded to refute every one of their mistaken beliefs, either by evidence, or simply by the proper application of a man's reason, a man such as Browne, who can adduce, for instance, that centaurs will have been first observed from a distance. These creatures were but ordinary horses, mounted and engaged in the activity of drinking—the heads and bodies of their riders in profile would be mistaken for their absented necks. Or, to take another, Orpheus did not make woods and trees follow the melody of his music. The bard, writes Browne, was merely passing a region in which various mad women lived who descended to the sound he made with boughs in their hands. And lastly, Medea only made men young again from knowledge of dyes and tinctures with which to apply the quality of youth to their hair.

Of the badger, writes Browne, not only those who have never seen one, so too those who have and may regularly hunt them, are each in the grip of a falsehood. Each wrongly claims the badger *hath legs on one side shorter then of the other.* This, Browne considers an affront to reason and *repugnant unto the course of Nature,* although he does report how the lobster can often have one claw longer than its counterpart, but these are not legs, properly speaking—the legs of the lobster are inverted backwards—and so this disequilibrium in the lobster is nothing near analogous to the falsely conceived limbs of the badger. Rather more, the claws of the lobster do form *a part of apprehension,* by which Browne presumably means that the lobster apprehends, that is to say seizes with its claws, and not that the creature reasons with them.

§

That Browne reasons on a flat plane is evidenced by his assumption that if the badger had shorter legs on one side, and longer legs on the other, it would run diagonal. Another decisive refutation, apparently.

Edward Topsell in his *Historie of Foure-footed Beastes* of 1607 has less trouble thinking aslant when he writes that the badger *runneth best when he getteth to the side of a hill, or a cart-road-way,* which makes sense of the differential limbs.

Topsell claims that when a badger has dug a fair way down and can no longer kick earth to the outside, any further earth is voided from the den by one badger falling upon its back, and another laying earth upon the upturned belly. When the barrow is fully laden, the second takes the hinder feet of the first in its mouth and pulls the belly-laden badger out and to the surface where it is disburdened.

§

OF FLOATING CORPSES, writes Browne, the common belief of how drowned women drift prone and men advance upon their backs, and that it occurs on the ninth day *when their gall breaketh,* is questionable on all counts. The time of putrefaction and corruptive gas-making depends on the season and the seasonable warmth, and so too on the fat of the body, given how cats and mice drowned at the same time will come to float at different points, as anyone who has observed the drowning of cats and mice will testify.

§

All demonstrable truths will have their chamber in the wall, or it is thinkable they might. At least following the age of science and empiricism and experiment they must. In this age and those thereafter multiple laboratories will exist within its recesses, unpeopled naturally, but mechanised, demonstrating repeatedly the veracity of their claims.

§

There is a laboratory for drowned animals where cats and mice are mechanically bred and reared and dropped into a tank at the same time and under different conditions to measure the effects.

§

There will surely be a tank, although I have not found it yet, in which Aristotle's claim that dead eels do not float is put to test.

§

And there will be a room in which the gall bladder is removed and still the little corpses float, and so it will be concluded, and demonstrably repeated, that the breaking of the gall, or its emissions, are not solely accountable for the floating.

Browne himself admits to removing the lungs of cats and mice to see if these are accountable for the floating, which they are not. And that he repeated the experiment with the guts and the bladder, and then perforated the cranium, and can report that the little creatures did again float, only it took them a while longer to do so.

§

It is a little-known fact that Browne directly killed more cats and mice than most other men of his generation in Norfolk if not in England. A century or so later this would have been difficult to boast. The residents of not so far away Leeds were alarmed in the year of 1760, and subsequently in 1763, and 1767, by the rising cry of rabid dogs and cats about town, whereupon notice was given by the magistrates *for all persons to confine their dogs, on pain of being destroyed.* The price was set at 12d a head for each cat or dog found on the streets, in consequence of which upwards of three hundred were killed, and their heads brought to the constables.

§

The season is now too hot for anatomical experiments, writes Browne to his first son in June of the year 1679. But if the occasion or opportunity offers itself, take notice of the penis of the cat, it is almost rough.

—in the year 1681, Browne returns to his earlier interests. As regard of the cat, tell me if its roughness might account for *the squeaking noyse they make in coitu.* And do see if you can get hold of a bear's penis too, for they are not difficult to secure possession of at a bear garden if bespoken, and tell me what it is like, for I doubt *whether a beares pizzle dryed bee more hard then that of a sea turtle—*

Later in the month of June 1679, Browne writes again in hopeful anticipation of better dissecting weather. When it *proves cold & fit for dissections,* and if you get the opportunity, take notice of the anatomy of the bear. Most of all examine its pectoral parts, for *tis commonly sayd that a beare hath no breast bone & that hee cannot well runne downe a hill* lest his heart come up to his throat. You should be able to find a specimen in London, I would have thought, or at least, you should be able to find a bear already submitting to the interests of somebody else, perhaps a taxidermist. Perhaps you should visit a taxidermist, for there you are sure to find a bear, or the remains of a bear, and might be able to take a look, first in the throat, and then the chest. I dissected a bear once myself, it died in Norwich, writes Browne, and have the lower jaw and teeth still to look at.

§

In 1681 there was a lengthy exchange between father and son concerning the latter's pet ostrich, recently procured, with much advice from the father concerning how the son should look after his bird, and what the son should look for concerning its behaviours and proclivities, and several times of how much the father looked forward to hearing of its dissection. This came soon enough. Browne was pleased with the account he was sent for its exactness, *but write not sceleton with a k,* writes father to son.

§

Browne had occasion to dissect a dolphin. He makes mention in a letter to his son. King Charles II was visiting Norwich at the time and seeing as *your mother hath an art to dresse & cooke the flesh so as to make an excellent savoury dish of it,* some quantity of dolphin was sent to his table. The King was reportedly well pleased with it. Browne confirms that its penis is only single, and not double as supposed.

In a subsequent letter from the year 1676, Browne enclosed the *ureters & bladder of a carp which wee had this day,* thinking his son might like it. The dried specimen was still preserved enough to be photographed for a new edition of Browne's letters originally issued in 1931, and then reissued more than a decade later. The book would have been volume six of The Works, only, volumes one to four were destroyed by enemy action in 1941, which meant the survivors, the two volumes entitled five and six, were no longer the fifth and sixth in the series, but were orphaned off *with the addition of a few errata.*

§

I send you the skin of a woman's palm, cast off at the end of a fever, writes Browne in the year 1679. I thought you might show it when giving your lecture on the skin for *it is neat & worthy to bee showne,* I would think. Snakes and lizards cast off their skins as a single piece, and diverse insects, and men do too by some diseases, *but I have not mett with any so neat as this; a palmister might read a lecture of it.* The whole soles of the feet came off too, by the by, *& I have one.*

§

I send you a few flies which in unhealthful years I have observed upon puddles in the marshes and in marsh ditches. *It were no hard matter to gather a peck of them.*

§

I send you a litle elegant sea plant, which I pulled from a greater bush thereof.

§

I send you the litle corpse of a sea fowle, called a sherewater, billed like a cormorant, feirce & snapping like it upon any touch.

—I kept 2 of them alive 5 weeks, cramming them with fish, but they were wont to refuse and so I wearied of cramming them, *& they lived 17 days without food.*

§

I send a ball taken out of the stomach of an ox, Browne writes his son, *and in the ball I send, there is one place opend where the hayre may be perceived.*

§

When you cut up slincks & abortives or pregnants, writes Browne to his son in another letter from another year, *you may observe how soon the hayre begins to appeare or bee any way discoverable upon the skin.* There is no comment—the observation appears to suffice as sufficient grounds for the cutting up.

—what rudiments you can discerne of the teeth in the jawes, which probably you thought not when you cut up the slinck.

§

Wee are all very sorry for the losse of the litle one, writes Browne to his son. And then somewhat bluntly—*The christening & buryalls of my children have cost mee above 2 hundred pounds & their education more; beside your owne which hath been more chargeable then all the rest putt together.* Advising his son lastly of all to save against an uncertain future, the letter switches back to their shared anatomical fixation. *Examine the spine of fishes & how the spinal marrowe is ordered in them*, the father recommends. Then comes mention of the cranium of a swan. It will be on its way soon from Norwich, Mr. Myngay intends for London next week and will bring it you there.

§

I hear there is an elephant in London, Browne writes his son again. *When you see the elephant observe whether hee bendeth his knees differently to other Quadrupeds*, the father asks, *& whether his belly bee the softest & smoothest part*, and if the testes *are not exterior & outward butt inwardly in the body*. And if you happen to see the dissection of the camel, be *good to observe of what that bunch in the back consisteth, whether the backbone or spine ariseth up into it, or it be a lump of flesh.*

—I thought good to give these hints, because probably they would not come into your mind.

Also, my hedgehogs have escaped with their young, Browne adds.

§

At least one chicken was killed, strangled Browne admits in his *Vulgar Errors*, this to test the common belief that men weigh more when dead. Having not a man to strangle, his evening meal was taken instead, the hen he was due to eat that night. This gave added interest to Browne's investigation of how much hen, his dinner, would be produced of the strangling.

It was found to be unchanged on the scales where it was by convenience dispatched. But when the hen had grown cold and several hours had elapsed a change did occur, though it was sensibly lighter—to Browne's chagrin, for he was hungry by now—and not heavier as might have been supposed.

The common belief had been refuted, which owes to the feeling and the false assumption of those who have carried the dead at the heaviness of a corpse—*I never knew him to be so heavy,* as so many have said. Browne's answer is forthright. The dead are only apparently heavier, and the living are only apparently lighter, since they will always in some way assist with the lifting, when assenting to it.

§

At least two frogs were killed by Browne, the first when testing the commonplace notion that a frog may be easily drowned, which Browne refuted by *fastning one about a span under water.* The unfortunate creature lived almost six days. Investigating further, Browne declares that the frog is not only hard to destroy under water, but so too on land, *for it will live long after the heart and lungs be out.* So much for the second frog.

§

The earwig may well have survived its inspection, during which Browne confirms that it does indeed have wings, and these may be prised out with a needle. So too the worm *dexterously pricked with a lancet* and which *emitteth a red drop.* It may have lived beyond Browne's interest. He was showing by pricking that the worm must not be placed, as so many have done, among the bloodless creatures.

Various flies and bees were less fortunate, following the ancient suggestion that bees in particular only buzz from one place, some have said of the wing, others from the mouth. Browne alternated between the cutting of wings and cutting off heads, to see which would kill the sound, only some did still buzz without a head, and others without their wings, and those *which are big and lively will hum without either head or wing.*

§

Of the pissing of toads Browne has several things to say, including the corrective, which is that toads, properly speaking, do not piss.

§

The famous antipathy between spiders and toads is tested— *having in a Glass included a Toad with several Spiders, we beheld the Spiders without resistance to sit upon his head and pass over all his body.* The indifferent toad declared against the myth.

§

Working backwards himself from the so-called *retromingency* or pissing-backward-habit of the hare, Browne thinks he can explain the common and peculiar belief that hares change sex. They must surely retrocopulate too, he claims, and this will explain the confusion of onlookers.

195

Meandering on to ancient rumours of women becoming men, and men becoming women, Browne decides they were all hermaphrodites from birth, and gives some way in so doing to the idea that Adam was the original hermaphrodite, and it is no accident that Genesis refers to Adam not as him but as them.

§

In a section on hens and their eggs, Browne measures the superiority of the Egyptians over the Babylonians in terms of their hatching abilities, since the former discovered how to hatch eggs in ovens, whilst the latter preferred *to roast them at the bottom of a sling, by swinging them round about, till heat from motion had concocted them.* The Babylonian approach was inferior in that it *confuseth all parts,* though Browne does not specify exactly what this meant, and if the chick lived, or if it did not how it looked, which must mean this was one test he did not see through to its conclusion. There is much Browne failed to refute by practical experiment, and he provides a list for ensuing plain-makers to follow and disprove.

—if the fasting spittle of a man be poison unto snakes and vipers.

—if the ostrich digesteth iron. Browne confesses he has not had the opportunity to experiment, even though *I have had sight of the Animal.*

—if mice may be bred by putrefaction, as has been suggested.

—if the poison of spiders may be cured against by music, and so on and etcetera.

§

What will he say to those rats and mice, or little beasts resembling mice found generated in the belly of a woman dissected after her death, writes Alexander Ross in regard of Browne's dismissal of the question of putrefaction, and of the idea that mice are bred of the decay of organics, and so not in the usual way, by mouse-to-mouse copulation.

—this appears in the *Arcana Microcosmi* of 1652, which contains a *Refutation of Dr Brown's* VULGAR ERRORS—

I have seen one whose belly, by drinking of puddle water, was swelled to a vast capacity, being full of small toads, frogs, evets, and such vermin, writes Ross.

There is no record of Browne mounting a counterclaim against his foe, by having women, or men for that matter, drink puddle water, and be as before demonstrably barren of small toads, frogs, newts, or other such vermin as a result of it. And this despite Ross going on and becoming quite positively inflated himself but with indignation.

—*so he may doubt whether in cheese and timber, worms are generated,* Ross continues, swelling still some, *or if beetles and wasps in cow's dung, or if butterflies, locusts, grasshoppers, shellfish, snails, eels, and such like, be procreated of putrefied matter, which is apt to receive the form of that creature to which it is by formative power disposed.*

To question this, is to question reason, sense, and experience, states

Ross in refutation of Browne, *let him go to Egypt, and there he will find the field swarming with mice begot of the mud of the Nile.*

§

If Browne has not fed iron to an ostrich, he has to a chicken, and can testify how *rusty Iron crammed down the throat of a Cock, will become terse and clear again in its gizzard.* This is not digestion, but corrosion.

§

Of the voracity of moles Browne speaks from experience, having enclosed a mole, a viper, and a toad in a glass and seen how the mole did dispatch and eat a good part of them both. If the viper and toad were to be replaced by their weight in worms, the size of that meal would be considerable and demonstrable of the underground appetite of the mole. That the mole did perish the day after is not thought worthy of attention, merely a mention, indicative as it otherwise might be that what occurred under the glass was not natural, but issued from the stresses of their confinement, and not from the mole's regular habits, as anyone might have observed in the contemporaneous gaols of London, where all manner of strange eating habits were consequent.

§

Of the mole lacking any eyes to speak of, Browne is at last indignant—*for that they have eyes in their head is manifest unto any that wants them not in his own.*

Errors are common in pictures too, writes Browne, and require correction, including the most abominable mistake of all, to depict Adam and Eve with navels.

Adam himself, in his entirety, must be properly thought of as a Navel. Adam was essentially this. There was, there could be no ligamental preference point by which he was connected to God and then sundered, not the end of the foot, nor the crown of his head. And thus—

All creatures are bound to their Maker in relations of elemental debt that course in from all directions about their surfaces. They are held in continuity even if they act themselves at a distance. And they are only let go at his pleasure. After this *they shall fall from their existence, essence, and operations: in brief, they must retire unto their primitive nothing, and shrink into their Chaos again.*

Browne introduces his own vulgar error, for he takes the umbilical cord as an evacuating member as well as a deliverer of nutriment. This evacuation is done, Browne claims, by the *Urachos or ligamental passage derived from the bottom of the bladder, whereby it dischargeth the waterish and urinary part of its aliment.* Browne's somewhat errant anatomy has consequence for the divine umbilical, entailing this—

ALL PISS was first directed at God and only secondly to the Earth.

§

§

There are many ways of coition, writes Browne. Worms couple sideways. Serpents do so circularly or by complication. Quadrupeds generally mount one another. Only Apes, Porcupines, and Hedgehogs approach one another pronely— the latter for obvious reason—and lastly, Crustaceous Animals, including Lobsters, Shrimps and Crevises—otherwise known as crayfish—do so aversly, alongside all retromingents, such as Panthers, Tygers and, of course, Hares. This is *the constant Law of their Coition*, and they observe and transgress it not.

—onely the vitiosity of man hath acted the varieties hereof; nor content with a digression from sex or species, hath in his own kind

200

run thorow the Anomalies of venery; and been so bold, not only to
act, but represent to view, the irregular wayes of Lust—

§

In the particular volume of *Pseudodoxia* found there in that
crevice was a note in pencil, *see for instance Seneca, Natural
Questions, Book I, Chapter XVI.* The import of which struck
me immediately. There were three possibilities.

FIRST, this volume of the *Pseudodoxia* had once been elsewhere
other than the here of the wall, and in this other place it had
been read and annotated upon.

SECOND, there must be, or have been, another wanderer in the
wall, who walked and read with a pencil.

THIRD, I myself had once wandered the wall with a pencil long
written away to its stump, or dropped, since I had none on my
person now.

Not one of these possibilities much changed the situation
before me. Or at least, assenting to the first, second, or third
possibility would not alter the challenge of finding Seneca's
Natural Questions somewhere in the recesses of the wall. The
books of the wall fall from no catalogue, nor do they come to
any order that might be recorded externally beyond the fact of
their stacking. They are classified architecturally, that is to say by
form and position, rather than notationally, which means that
the books are distributed spatially without a bibliographic trace
or the chance of taking one. Within a relatively small chamber

the shelves can be navigated with time, whereas in the larger chambers the quantity of books, and the incorporation of minor arches, and buttresses, and the inevitable recesses, reduce transit between one book and another to a matter of whimsy. So too is the question of transit between chambers. It is done more or less at random. In the ideal I might chance upon a room in which the bookish remains of Seneca specialists would be gathered together, arranged in their shared obsessive poverty and lodged with Seneca's greater remains. Or, alternatively, I would find Seneca's book in a room devoted to Sadean Man that would include Sade's precursors, and so would shelve the exploits of Heliogabalus, the teenage emperor, as they were variously recorded—including Artaud's account of the emperor's short, violent, and uniquely erotic reign. This book by Artaud will be in the wall even centuries before Artaud was born, lived, and died, a poet withered to his unshrinking substrate—and then perhaps in a corner I would find a few pages of Seneca's *Book I, Chapter XVI*, which is really very tame and stringently devoid of specifics. In any case, I did eventually come to a copy of *Natural Questions* and read about Hostius Quadra and his mirrors. These were so adjusted that small things became abnormally large. A finger, to take a comparatively chaste example, might exceed the size of an arm in length and thickness. And a toe might grow so big as a head, but faceless and ill shod with hair. With these mirrors, and with Hostius Quadra at their centre, *he could see all his accomplices' movements, and could gloat over the imagined proportions of his own body. He raised a levy of scamps like himself in all the public baths*, writes Seneca, and this only *whetted his appetite to have his scenes of riot reproduced in false unnatural proportions.* And it goes on, with Seneca repeating himself over and again concerning its baseness, its lewdness, its shamelessness, all in place of any particulars. *I could not soil my pen by recording the foul words and deeds of that monster*, is written instead. Seneca describes more than once how the mirrors were placed on all sides so to present infamy from all aspects, and how these were all *deeds of darkness* which ordinary men would balk at, retch at, turn from, and so on, crimes that would usually and even for the most debauched cause the doer to dread the sight of themselves, abominations that would drag heavily at the last vestiges of a conscience. All of which were but a trifle still to this beast. And Seneca goes on with his circular telling of scenes of revolting iniquity, a convolution of sentences wound in their own filament of judgement. One angle alone could not satisfy his lust, and so each deed must be seen from below, and behind, and from every side, *he had no dread of the daylight,* no repugnance before what he might do, and more likely felt disappointment that whatever it was he did could not be seen enough, nor magnified sufficiently, for the image to reproduce in its grotesque distortion how they each felt in their bodies, or at least how Hostius Quadra felt in his when in the court of their debauchery all accepted notions of the manner of human coitus were disploded, and as the entire evaluative order was rent between them, since this was how he experienced it, and perhaps too those he debauched with, and so it was, this villain *presented to his sight what the darkest night is not deep enough to hide.* Which might be interpreted then to mean, the reflected image would always fail to fully render something more bestial, elemental, that purest darkness, even, could not conceal. The mirrors distorted body parts and separated them out, and Hostius Quadra feasted upon them. As he feasted himself on the parts presented, he saw himself engorging them in his reflection, and this was the closest any man ever got to feasting his eyes upon an image, to bearing out the common phrase thereby, and to finally replacing the operation of the eye with the sensation of the mouth. This will be achieved by masticating the image, making it whetted and malleable and enlarged as it feels against the tongue and the gums and the palate. The oracular feast will begin here, placing the eye between the lips and sucking in and to a painful endenture, a blunt compression of teeth that brings the organ into a grasp of its nature—a jellied orb distended and overrun with sensitivities. Seneca concludes his vignette by allowing the monster to speak, or at least, Seneca ends by giving him words to speak with. Seneca does this as a narrative ploy for the purposes of burrowing under and undermining those apportioned words, so taking the debauchee down with his own locution. *By my art I will defeat nature's shyness,* says the man of the mirrors. *Nature is more generous to cattle…* than men, Hostius Quadra adds. Men must rail against the smallness nature bequeathed them, against the frailty of the human form, and against its further enfeeblement by the refinements of culture. But this last clause just added, and the one before, and then before that reaching right back to the quoted text, already extends beyond what Seneca permits. For Seneca cannot allow the abominations he hints at to suggest by their fabled existence, by their apparent achievement and their reflected glory, that nature was in any way defeated in the chamber of distorting mirrors. The episode must in its last be reduced to a story of failure. This has to be done for the opening line of *Book I, Chapter XVI* to be concluded and so delivered in the last words of the passage. The section must make good on its claim that this will be a salutary tale against lust. *I wish to tell you a little story to show you how unscrupulous lust is in seizing every instrument that will rouse passion, so resourceful is it in goading to madness its own morbid fury*, is how Seneca begins. The beast himself will be made to confess, tell of his failure to defeat nature, and show that he was himself seized by lust against himself and was diminished in its grasp. *I only wish I could make the size real,* Seneca has him say of the grotesque and magnified reflection Hostius Quadra beholds, *but I must be content with the belief of it,* or as differently translated, *I will feed upon the lie,* or again, rendered differently, *I will feed myself with the similitude.* After all the lewdness, or the suggested lewdness, the monster is reduced to a man, and the man is reduced to his wish to be what he sees, what he has conjured by common trickery, and so to his desire to be what he is not. The debauchee is made small before his reflection. The image is elevated against the man, and not the man before the image that must perpetually fail him, that cannot reproduce him, because the man is always more faceted, and worse in relief, than a mirror, or a mirror-like image can capture.

§

When the men woke from their hollows, and if they did not outright return to sleep, they crawled across the earth for the sight of their reflections in the gathered wetness.

§

And when they saw their image after six months alone with the memory of a face that had lost its contours with time and twilight, where colour drains and edges soften, the merest ripple in their puddle struck them to start upwards, and remove backwards, and then they thereupon bellied overland to another reflecting pool not yet moved.

§

It is believed that when a pond-skater skirmishes across a face reflected in a pond, if the face has dimples, they will diminish with age, whereas if a boatman paddles across the mouth, it will forget and misplace words and stutter as the oars of the insect stroke the water.

§

It is not difficult to best Browne in plain-making, particularly for those who, in subsequent centuries, learned that the art of criticism hangs on the arrogance of the critic.

—when Browne refutes at length the so-called existence and subsequent belly-walking antics of the two-headed Amphisbaena, he misses the more obvious objection. The falsity of the Amphisbaena resides, as Browne does not notice, in the simple fact there is debate among believers about which is the leading head, a debate that hangs on deciding which way is forward. But if the creature has two heads at opposite ends and submits one head to trail when the other moves forward, and the other head to trail when it moves backward, it will neither know backward nor forward, nor can it be known by its backward and forward motions. There can simply be no backward or forward, and so no Amphisbaena. If the rumours concerning its existence spoke of this way and that, of one head trailing this way and the other leading that, the existence of the creature might be more easily believed. Or if there were other anatomical features, perhaps feet, that declared front and back, the Amphisbaena might once again exist, only it would now live subservient to its feet, and this Browne would presumably not allow either, given the creature is known for its two heads, and not for its feet. Yet Browne gathers other evidence, or argument which counts as evidence, and points to the lack of a similar creature in nature, even if nature does permit some strangeness at times, such as the Buzzard with three testicles that Aristotle himself testifies to handling.

§

Snakes give birth by erupting and expiring from the belly, or so it is said, and as Browne will say, it makes no sense to have said so. This death by birth would upturn and frustrate the benediction of God who blessed his creatures and bid them go forth and multiply.

Some reason of it can be made, nonetheless, he adds, if the viper is accursed as the original Serpent was itself accursed before Adam and Eve. God's blight upon the Woman, *IN SORROW SHALT THOU BRING FORTH*, can be extended to the viper. And God's curse upon the Serpent, *UPON THY BELLY SHALT THOU GO AND DUST SHALT THOU EAT ALL THY LIFE*, can be extended to the Woman. These are both of them belly folk. The men who slept six months of the year were belly folk too and might be having a little of the accursed Woman and the Serpent about them.

§

When they rouse and rake through the muck, the men from the holes make what they see from the materials around them. This is called work. Only when asleep is there liberation for the production of intangibles with no relation to the demands of the roused and raking.

§

There was a rumour among them that a library can reside in a fingernail, and with fingers and toes combined they carried twenty libraries apiece. This library must be extraordinarily compact, they thought, or else they must be giants. Not knowing which hardly mattered when they could not see it in any case.

§

Another held a library in the folds of his foot. Still another in the back of a tooth.

§

Nothing is written for those not yet existent—even if they, when driven to consider what was written before them, think otherwise—and little is produced for those who are. Everything is written for those time has fled.

—everything is written *from those* whose time has fled, he said, correcting himself.

All things were written for the celestial wanderer to see, laid up on a methane dune beyond the orbit of Neptune. He could easily boast to have a library anywhere—in a tooth, fold of a foot or fingernail included, should that have been his fancy.

Much like can be imagined with the wanderer merely exchanging a chariot for a ship and it being either chariot or ship depending which century it was when I returned to the wall and its temporal anomaly. When the chariot was extant, he lay on the dune itself after the journey, unprotected, disrobed, not much perturbed by the lack of air, and may have stridden from planet to star but for the distances. If reclining, when reclining, the anatomy of the calf and the foot were muscular outriders. If there were a robe, the thigh would be out, and if there were none, the severely penned lines continued up the legend and round the torso, these lines having no patience for the typical profile of a body that is smooth or at best wrinkled or puckered. Those smoother bodies are of no interest to a pen that trained itself upon mountain vistas where the soil has receded or never grew, their skins taut over underlying and cropped rock. That was the basis of the celestial figure, as pictured, with the training of the pen suitable to his proportions, definite to its lines, and to those of the dune. His elbows rested and when they shifted left craters—not that these themselves were drawn—and the figure had no cause to wonder how the air in its thinness could take sand particles and then pile them to produce his recumbency. There was no atmosphere depicted, indeed the lack of it was not thought.

Plutonian winds may encircle the planet in a fleet of hours, or days, the question is indifferent. They drop into its plains and climb over its mountains, vapid and lacking in ferocity but quick. Storms which travel a hundred miles per hour feel like gentle breezes. A wind speed which would flatten a forest on earth cannot pick up nor entrain particles of their own initiative. Mountains are capped and their ledges are layered over, but with methane ice. It does not snow upon them or anything else, excepting in winter when the entire atmosphere near enough falls to the ground. A Plutonian year is long, not a fraction of a season may be observed in a lifetime, and much of the Plutonian circuit—a quarter millennium—remains purest supposing. How the mountains are capped, how the dunes form, supposition all of it. Suppose then this, said they, a final haze at the outer fringe intercepts the light. The surface by way of that haze is even colder than it should otherwise be. Yet a quantum of heat makes it down, little packets of energy tracked through space to a place with small gravity, and against its weakness particles fly up when struck and course awhile through the aether. Some drop to rest on high places—the Plutonian massif—loaf about, then get lofted from those peaks, gather in plains, and roll over from their ballistic hops to cumulate as dunes. Somewhere below the dunes, perhaps an ocean, even languid water, thick and near frozen, causing the crust to show of it, flexed or cracked, the ancient shear marks evidence of oceanic convection kept warm by gravitational flexing from a nearby moon. They call her Charon.

But these were the estimates of a subsequent age. Before, and when dunes were mere feints and not observable or nameable, stranger things were said.

For instance, the dune was starlit when tilted to the sun and was like any other dune on earth in composition. It was difficult to see how sand could blow here or imagine the breath of the wind without hanging a kingfisher from an unwound thread to serve its direction. In a draft-free room the bird points its breast to the horizon and tells how the wind directs outside. So why not hang the bird over the comparatively airless surfaces of Pluto. Its sensitivities are requisite.

The absurdity known as the jointless elephant will take to Pluto too, riding on its *pillars of flesh*, fleeing a hostile earth and the refutations of Browne who declares such a creature cannot exist. If the elephant has no joints, it cannot sit, says Browne, just as seven elephants once sat, or reputedly sat, dressed like women and clad like men, drinking and eating very mannerly. The jointless elephant cannot walk on ropes *in publick shews before the people*, or follow Hannibal across the alps, even if he made a passage by softening its rocks with a vinegar concoction.

§

The jointless elephant will stand on Pluto without sitting and will have nothing to say. Unlike on earth where there is much to say and considerable air to say with.

§

That some Elephants have not only written whole sentences, but have also spoken, we do not conceive impossible, writes Browne. Having no elephants at hand to watch, and failing that, to dissect, Browne must rely on the ancients.

The elephant is sensitive beyond all other animals and *to a degree that is rare among men,* writes Pliny. It is susceptible to the pleasures of love and glory, and holds *in religious reverence and with a kind of devotion not only the starres and planets, but the sunne and moone.*

§

The Plutonian elephant has Charon to look at, a looming orb. The sun nothing much from this distance.

§

Stationed on its pillars of flesh, Pluto's elephant regards the wanderer reclining on his dune and wonders what he sees when picking his teeth, or the folds of his feet, and his fingernails too. Standing there below him, Pluto's elephant might even give man's presence little or no regard at all, finding the rest of Pluto rather more telling of its universe.

§

The elephant has a deep sense of justice, writes Pliny, referring here only to the Earth elephant, and not the Plutonian.

King Bocchus bound thirty elephants to a stake and compelled another thirty to blunder and wreak vengeance against them.

Yet no matter how much they were prickled and provoked by their keepers, not one could be convinced to execute his butchery or be ministers of another's cruelty.

In Rome these creatures were initially known as *Lucanian Oxen*, as they had first been observed in Lucania, in Southern Italy.

Before they were put to work, and then to war, elephants were exhibited in the circus, and eventually slain with javelins for want of a better method of disposal. Not much had travelled with the elephant, by this account, beyond its physical presence in Lucania, and this was how the elephant arrived at Pluto, the jointless one, with no memory or accompanying story of the jointed ones that slaved away well beyond the knowledge of Rome. Or, when not enslaved, fought dragons. And when not fighting dragons, defeated flies by swiftly contracting their reticulated skin. The flies were trapped and died by compression.

§

The elephant is *a living Mountain*, writes Topsell, still looking aslant and otherwise much plagiarising Pliny.

The elephant is *not without all Motion*, writes Browne.

The elephant is *easily clasped by dragons*, writes Pliny.

India *bringeth forth the biggest*. These wind around them easily *and withal tie them fast with a knot*. Both dragon and elephant die in consequence. The elephant falls down dead just as conquered,

*and with his heavie weight crusheth and squeaseth the dragon that
is wound and wreathed about him.*

They say the blood of the elephant is refreshingly cool, writes
Pliny. The dragon lusts after it, clasps on, drinks all of the
contents of the elephant which, sucked dry, falls down once
more, *and the dragons again, drunken with their blood, are squised
under them, and die both together.*

—plain-makers may say that the dragons were serpents, and
the serpents were boas, and that the blood of the elephant is
not particularly refreshing after all, which will in most cases
be supposition still.

§

The Poets, writes Topsell, compare true dreams to horn and
false dreams to ivory. This is explicable, for the *eye of man is
translucent and containeth in it a horny substance,* whereas the
mouth contains teeth and so lays closer to the substance of
ivory. Thus it be *by the eye we always receive the best assurance,*
whereas by the mouth *many falsehoods are vented.* Moreover,
horns point upward to heaven, whereas ivory points to the
earth, *the mother of error,* and from the earth to the below-earth,
whereunder even error ceases to gain purchase.

§

The Plutonian elephant knows about horns and truth and ivory
and lies, having overheard the celestial wanderer read Topsell's
bestiary from a crevice in the side of his thumb.

Since then, and ever more after, the creature points its tusks indifferently at the horizon, which is neither heaven nor earth.

Man would rather grow horns and falsify with them, and tell truths with teeth clasped upon an eyeball, the elephant might have said.

§

If an elephant devours a chameleon the creature will perish unless it straight after consumes a wild olive, writes Topsell. Which is to say, the elephant will perish. The chameleon is clearly done for.

§

The elephant will only drink wine during times of war and does so to drunkenness. Otherwise it prefers muddy water from a natural loathing of its reflection.

§

The elephants of antiquity were trapped by a multitude of devices—each one a subterfuge beyond the imaginings of the brute. Including entrapment by night, for instance, in a craftily concealed enclosure. Those fleeing were slain against bent spears, those remaining gradually starved to weakness. These were then run over by tame elephants driven at their shrunken bellies. And then fettered as they threshed about on their sides, and watched from a distance as they rose and fell again from the unexpected constraint. Next bridled, with straps of raw ox hide, and tied to those already defeated by a previous entrapment, and then ridden and subdued in their attachment. The rider, now protected, cuts the skin of the neck round about in a circle with a sword, and over the wound ties a rope that shall be its halter. Eventually the beast is convinced of its weakness, writes Topsell, and leaves off with its wildness, leaving off again and again from that wildness in a recurrent infliction of man's will from one century to the next. Many of these elephants, weakened, un-wilded, were driven out to man's killing fields, *some having their knees and bones broken, other their eyes trod out of their head, other their noses pressed flat to their faces, and their whole villages so disfigured and disfavoured in a moment, that their nearest friends, kindred and acquaintance cannot know them.* After which violences the culminating feat of elephant training is to teach the elephant to write, *how to frame the letters* first, and then to *follow the true proportions of the characters expressed before their face, whereupon they look as attentively as any Grammarian.*

§

The elephant has more than once served its absent master by climbing atop the conjugal bed to crush both adulterer and adulteress in one decisive enouncement, writes Topsell.

§

Susceptible to the beauty of women, the elephant wooed the very same woman as Aristophanes who saw its trunk deliver apples to her bosom. The playwright straight conceded to his rival. The woman meant little enough to Aristophanes, or to those who told the anecdote, that she remains unnamed and joins all the nameless, faceless existences, which function as the human bustle, the objective meat, the social surround of historic man. She meant less still to the elephant, something Aristophanes himself could not imagine. Even in the diminished world of its captivity she had no purchase on the creature and did not pierce its unfathomable muteness. Within the wall the books I read did not pierce it, even in that room which in later centuries was dedicated to the elephant, the mastodon, and the mammoth, and would subsequently contain reports of attempts to revive the latter from its multiple burials in the permafrost.

§

The mastodon—an extinct elephant-like mammal named for the nipple shaped tubercules on the crowns of its molar teeth, I read.

§

The mammoth—an extinct elephant-like mammal, known to subsequent imaginaries as a victim of rudimentary, stone-tipped spears. And then thereafter known of by extractions from syringe-pierced necrotic flesh and subsequent acculturation to the womb of its distant, domesticated and comparatively hairless divergent.

§

We owe a considerable debt to palaeolithic man—it is written— for assembling so many specimens of the megafauna in their kill sites, making easy work for the excavators and representatives of knowing. The beasts lie piled or close enough for those with brushes and spades and scrapers to merely roll from one ancient carcass to another, and this they do merely for the thrill of it. Years and miles may usually separate one oversized bear, or beaver, or sloth, from the next, with the exception of the pre-historic kill site at which palaeontologists do sometimes also dance a little, in a cumbersome sort of way, although this too is discouraged and diligently atoned for with all the methodical scraping and brushing they subsequently do. The gradualism of exhumation is not always necessitated yet will be performed for the killing of enthusiasms it affords, that any science worthy of the name will need to carefully manage. Listened to up close, the brush and the brush return, its stroke and reply, intones the words *hush now, hush now, hush now,* a message directed at the very soul of the scientist. The contrasting sounds of those who first worked at the site, and still had flesh to tear, would have been less quieting. These might be read as the longest-running collaborations in the history of science—a fancy that—spanning a minimum ten thousand years from first to last author. Given the time elapsed, it is necessarily impossible to cite the first collaborators in their work of assemblage by butchery. Their citational practices were rudimentary in any case—cut lines in the bone—and they did not anticipate us. The dry exactitudes of palaeontology, an entirely bone-ridden science, are derivative of the subject matter with its absence of meat, and skin, and sinew, and there is no comparative requirement to overcome the viscera that modern day medics, and anatomists, must first train as the ground of dispassion. Something of the palaeolithic kill site survives in the modern slaughterhouse, just as something of the slaughterhouse is remaining on the surgeon's lap. Palaeontology is less prone to wet ingress, more amenable to dry analysis, owing itself to the prior evisceration of its materials once performed by those who would also and somewhat inevitably become its subjects.

§

The wandering intelligence of a modern-day laboratory worker will alight on the desiccating jars found sitting on the window shelves, their arid atmospheric trapped under heavy lids, the ground joint lubricated to suction, held by more than weight even without the applied vacuum.

A future writer, Georges Bataille, does link the development of intelligence to the drying up of life.

Intelligence was set in place on the condition of being and making arid, on the basis that moist interiors—a watery brain but the other organs too—were places within which intelligent functions might become lost.

Or was it that the intelligence grew from the body in the manner of a fungal rupture, a dry rot. Something inside the brain became parched, attracted to fixed points, yet cracked in the manner of shrinkage of wet indeterminates, or moist intermediaries, otherwise seen on lake beds, desert floors, and cracked palms.

Future suspicions, all of these. But the line, Bataille's line, linking the development of intelligence to the drying up of life, may still be found before him in the wall. The line will exist before it was owned, as all lines pre-determine themselves. Bataille's words can be read long in advance insofar as Bataille's words apply to worlds before they were written.

Or, more accurately, Bataille's words may be found in the wall long before the man known as Bataille was born, but only to the extent they would be understood in those worlds.

Here then, and on this basis, on the question of their prior application, and on the chance of their advance decipherment, can Bataille's line and some other Bataillean words be seen to exist, existing in the abridged form future books may take when inhumed years or even centuries before they were written.

The so-called objective writers have no such prehistory.

§

For an early plain-maker, Browne's experiments were decidedly wet, and his furniture was notoriously watermarked. Or so it was said between those whose job was to clear up after and then serve the juiciest meats and the better wines. Upon these propulsions Browne returned with renewed vigour to the next watermark-making dissection. The Norwich cats and mice he drowned to test the effects of fats upon the buoyancy of the corpse, or the hen Browne wrung out to see if the dead really do weigh more than the living, or the frogs he fastened below water for days to see if they could survive, or the surviving frog that lasted awhile with its lungs and heart strung out to show how hard after all they are to kill, or the worm Browne pricked with a lance to see if it could bleed, or the toad, viper and mole trapped in their swift-condensing hostilities to see which would kill the others, or even the flies and bees which had their wings plucked and their heads prised off to hear from where they buzzed. Insects may appear crisp but have their own juices—and Browne to his merit, remained moist in the brain.

§

The celestial wanderer had occasion to clean out his fingernails. And flicked. Books went here and there about the surfaces of Pluto, several of these finding lodging in the reticulated skin of the elephant. This elephant, since returned to earth, is housed within the wall inside a cathedral-like chamber, or a chamber which might easily house a cathedral. The creature is much dried up and despite its size and jointlessness otherwise resembles those still found within the retreating permafrost. Some particles of methane sand remain within the crevices of its skin, which, when parted, pass wind. The volumes once flicked inside may also be retrieved, page by page, with terrarium or long-handled tweezers, and so read, such as Lucian's *Charon, or the Inspectors*, which tells of the journey the ferryman takes to earth, wishing to understand why so many tears are dropped from the sides of his craft as the dead are taken down under on their way to Hades. When he sees how utterly appalling life on earth can be, Charon remains perplexed. Why might anyone regret leaving it—seems odd—the depth of the human tear duct, inexplicable.

§

What are you laughing at, says Hermes, on first seeing Charon. I am laughing at the sight of what is called human living, Charon replies, and the accident, the senselessness of what they call dying, he adds.

—a tile falls off a roof and kills a dinner guest outright, right after promising his host he will be back tomorrow. Charon's laughter is simple—

But the ferryman's laugher deepens as he sees more of their living and their dying. It becomes cavernous, a belly ache not dissimilar from the movements of the earth's crust, of the mantle, this perceptive, proximate laughter, of a trip into knowing the feeling they call loss, into a fuller understanding of their surfaces, a perception that does not apprehend, or arrest, but strays into the feeling it seeks to know. With heaven debarred, it must be done from a high mountain, only, Caucasus, Parnassus, and Olympus will not do when it is possible to pluck the mountain of Ossa from its base, and roll it atop Olympus, and then set Pelion atop both, and Oeta and Parnassus upon them thereafter. It cannot be all that hard, Hermes thinks, if Homer can pile two mountains across a pair of verses, one mountain above another, so easy as that. And with Parnassus having two peaks, there will be a seat for each.

I see tiny little men, says Charon, and things which look like their hiding places. Those things you call hiding places are cities, Hermes replies.

Having received some enchantments to the eyes and their benefit for his seeing, peering down from the height of not one mountain top but five, Charon looks more closely at the tiny little men and develops a better understanding of their heedlessness.

Burn them, says he, *cut off their heads and crucify them, so that they may know that they are human. In the meantime let them be exalted, only to have a sorrier fall from a higher place. For my part I shall laugh when I recognize them aboard my skiff.* Thus, Charon learns to laugh as humans do, with a sense of their tragedy, of how they construct their lives as tragedy.

Then Hermes describes the manner in which all beings are attached to slender threads extending upward. These threads are their fates. And how they are entangled together by them, some lifted at times high above the ground, but for a moment, and when falling downward, as the thread breaks, they make great noise, whereas others are lifted but a little, and when they fall crash so noiselessly they are scarcely noticed in their dying.

All this is very funny Hermes! replies the ferryman, returning to this earlier, simpler mirth.

§

In another fold of reticulated skin, Lucian's *Icaromenippus, or the Sky-Man,* in which, and from the vantage of the moon, Menippus peers into men's houses and spectates their lives—all of it found wanting, lowly, grubby.

So too from that fold of skin will emerge René Lesage's *The Devil on Two Sticks.* Again—yet so many centuries later—the onlooker spectates into houses. All roofs in Madrid are as if removed, and he laughs, and judges, and laments.

In each book, there is really very little distancing done at all, merely a show of distance, a comedy of distances. Despite what is written, Menippus never makes it to the moon, not even out of the city, and Lesage's young Spaniard scarcely leaves his own bed, toilet, and table.

And then, another such book. Found about the ankle, or thereabouts, where the folds of elephantine skin are especially deep and calloused over. From this recess I retrieved an edition of Voltaire's MICROMEGAS, wherein the giants, Sirian and Saturnian, are so huge, and humans so comparatively tiny, they scarcely exist. Mere atoms, really, these men were of such miserable proportion it was hard to imagine they could think, or that they might each have a soul, or that they were anything other than *bordering indeed on annihilation.*

Should a grenadier hear of man's inspection by the giants he would surely raise his troopers' hats by at least two feet, but it would be pointless. All human action is played out at the level of insignificance, even the actions of those with taller hats.

At worst, these little satires deploy distance as a facile tool—height is the basic metaphor of a criticism which refuses to consider its own enmirement.

At best, they tell of such heights, of flights to high places, and of distanced, downward looking inspections, to ridicule their more serious cousins—the philosopher or poet who writes in all solemnity of lofty places, of soaring wisdoms and elevated points of view. As such, they blow their own breezes at the conceits of spiritual uplift, or the pretensions of high objectivities, or clarities, or purities of judgement, attained by all the real or imagined flights of their poesy.

True criticism, thought I, said he—or so it was written in the flyleaf of MICROMEGAS—*is written across the scar*, or upon a weal, or under a flap of skin, or from out of the mud.

§

The Plutonian giant gnawed awhile on his thumbnail out of which popped *Doorways of Primitives*, though he was actually thinking, for that moment, of a different book— MICROMEGAS—in which Voltaire describes how the thinking atoms eventually measured the Sirian giant by sticking a ranging pole in a hole *that Dr Swift would have mentioned quite explicitly*, namely, his arse.

§

Rummaging in the region of his breeches, the Plutonian giant came across the little volume he had been looking for since growing tired of thinking about Voltaire, a book entitled *Doorways of Primitives*, which he read aloud but without much interest, wishing instead for something to gnaw on. The basic argument of the book, which concerns the avoidance of verticals in primitive doorway constructions, would have struck the Plutonian as singularly narrow and besides irrelevant to one residing on a planet without doorways, excepting his own metaphorical equivalents, and those of the jointless elephant, which again, *Dr Swift would have mentioned quite explicitly.*

This caused the Plutonian to ruminate a little on his excremental function, and the various arguments that have been levelled at the primacy of that function in man's experience.

Including the suggestion that excretion is *the primal act of revolt and repudiation of the past,* which for the Plutonian was all too neat and symptomatic.

And then the suggestion that it is *the bodily archetype of spiritual rebirth insofar as it liberates the body from itself.* Again, the Plutonian was not convinced.

A more intriguing formula is the following—

If shitting is a consummate pleasure, it begins, *this is because at a certain moment free will and necessity, what one wants and what one must, precisely coincide.*

This to say, with the act of shitting, will is expired in necessity. Or as the formula is re-stated, and somewhat reformulated—

The art of shitting well momentarily frees the body from, even as that body joyfully succumbs to, its anal curse.

Or reformulated again—

In the moment of excremental release, the body is for a short bit discharged of the burden of an alternately worrisome, overweening, overlord.

—the Plutonian giant had enough of all this and examined his crevices for something else to think with.

§

Against the conceit that of all God's creatures, only men stand erect, and this is what predisposes them to behold heaven, Browne rejoins, but what of the penguin of which Magellan speaks, and besides, *Man hath a notable disadvantage in the Eye lid; whereof the upper is far greater then the lower, which abridgeth the sight upwards.* Should the anatomy of men predispose them to heavenly seeing, they would shut their eyes as birds do, with the lower lid advancing upward and the upper lid scarce shifting down. Actually, this conceit would be swiftly disploded if those who held it looked for one moment at the Uranoscopus, or Beholder of Heaven, a fish which cannot but gaze upwards, and looks, like many of the uglier fish, as if it might have been another one of God's mistakes.

§

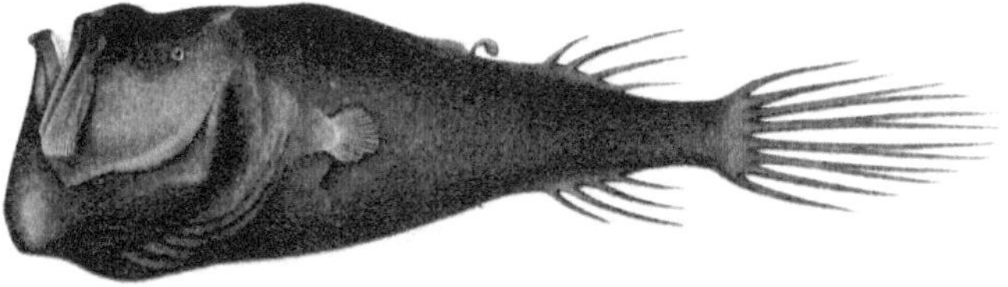

Anaximander claimed that humans first emerged from a fish, or fish-like creature, inside which the first little clutch of foetuses first grew and were retained until they reached puberty. After that they were promptly expelled. Men and women crawled out, and were able to feed themselves, perhaps beginning with their surrogate.

§

The illegitimacy of all men and women, of the great injustice of their having come into existence as they did, is something they must atone for, repeatedly, by death and return to the boundless. Or so Anaximander seems to suggest. This is a fate all creatures share, and indeed all things. All existences must atone for themselves, where returning to the boundless, by either dying or simply by ceasing to exist as a determinate something, is the penance they owe. The joke of it is in the very juice of using words such as justice and injustice in relation to such aboriginal contexts, which was how Anaximander made a mockery of his aboriginal thinking. But what if the birth of humans can only be thought of by later humans, by the civilized, in their own terms, and what if Anaximander's original clumsiness here, is also his telling wisdom.

The first humans emerged with all the trappings, or if not the trappings, all the dispositions of a civilized being, and so came forth with the capacity to indulge its basic pessimism. This is the judgement it makes when deciding that all things are a mistake. All things were a mistake, the civilized say in the moment of their severest pessimism. And by proclaiming this, believe themselves capable of passing sentence on all things, which means that the moment of the greatest loss of faith is also the moment of its greatest exertion, and the moment of severest objectivity is the moment of its surest failure. It turns out that Anaximander was very close to the nub of his problem, and that the truest thing one could say remains the thing that Anaximander almost said, which is that the *civilized* emerged from the belly of a fish, and not the first humans.

§

The vast quarters assigned to the Plutonian elephant are set alongside a much smaller chamber containing a large fish caught in 1546, or thereabouts, resembling a monk. It floats fully clothed in a tank of dark seawater, surrounded by all mentions of its existence in printed and written form, including multiple woodcuts divergent in their anatomies and first appearing in the 1550s. So too for consultation will be seen the original sketches, drawn from life, or from over the corpse. These sketches may or may not have been seen by the woodblock cutters, but whichever way were drawn, or at least first transported, by respectable and trustworthy persons. Or so it was said.

From the centuries that followed its discovery are stacked about the tank several attempts to explain away the supposed existence of the sea monk as a case of mistaken identity. These correctional writs against fancy will be made by those looking across the animal kingdom for any and all creatures that might resemble a monk found drowned at sea and dressed in a waterlogged habit. The monkfish is mentioned as a likely contender—presumably the flattened shark which goes by that name, and not the far more repellent looking sea devil, or sea-frog, of the genus *Lophius*—but also the giant squid was thought a fitting match, and somewhat inexplicably, the angler fish with its lure and gaping mouth. The monkfish, or *Squatina squatina*, has in addition to its name, other notably monk-like features. Its pectoral fins might be the sleeves of the waterlogged member emerging from under the chasuble and the other waist level vestments. And the pelvic fins would be the rest of the cloth flapping heavily below the girdle. Its bald nose would be the tonsure, or perhaps the cowl, and the nostrils of the fish, evidently the eyes. But then, the giant squid figures well too in its outer trappings, with its mantle also resembling the vestments of a monk, particularly when the creature is stranded above water, which is when the squid becomes flaccid. An even more fitting match for the squid could be imagined than a mere monk, however, with the mantle now resembling a mitre, and so it was that a sea bishop was also found in another sea at another time. The arms of the sea monk would be formed easily enough from the appendages of the squid, if the two longer tentacles were folded, laid under the body of the mantle, and presented only at their tips from below the edges of the body as if emergent there. If the sea monk did survive a little while after being caught, this does not rule out the giant squid or the monkfish as viable hypotheses. Each could live a short time out of water, although the monkfish perhaps would appear to survive longer, given that its mouth parts can be moved and be made to gape, and snap shut, by crafty manipulation. This little collection about the tank includes a letter from King Christian III of Denmark to the Holy Roman Emperor then residing in

Spain. It still bears the tired impatience of its recipient Emperor in its broken wax seal. The contents of the letter detail the catch, and reassure the old universalist, who was about to meet his own death—in his bed, holding a cross, and not dredged up from the seabed by a hook—that the sea monk had not said a word against the empire, nor against its God, and that it did not snub the emperor either, even if it could not exactly be declared in his favour. And lastly, if it murmured something of a realm beyond his conquering, it said nothing specific about that unconquered place. This would be good enough for a depleted imperialist who cannot bear stories of places not under his yoke. *It lived for three days, so I am informed*, the King wrote his Emperor. Adding then this assurance—*and produced no sounds except deep expirations or sighs.*

§

After leaving the sea monk I came across another, larger room containing every single Jenny Haniver ever produced by mutilating and mummifying the carcass of a ray. These were hung at intervals so that the breeze of a visitor would cause them to shudder.

§

And in another the sea bishop of 1531 floating in its own tank of dark seawater, the latter perhaps also drawn up from the deep of the same century, and so, showing the sea as it was, in that time, and at that depth.

§

And a room filled with skulls of the so-called crucifix fish of South America. Each skull contains a little crucified figure when viewed from the underside, with two small bones known as the Weberian ossicles forming a halo. When shook, the otoliths, or ear bones, rattle inside, and the visitor can walk from one skull to the next, and hear each martyr rattle it out. Many have been daubed with paint to enhance the realism, although those that remain unpainted, and are bleached by the sun, or stained by handling, suggest better the harsh hand clutched realism of crucifixion. The upper surface of the skull meanwhile resembles a hooded monk with outstretched arms, or the breastplate of a Roman soldier, but when the skull is broken so that the bones of the head may be separated, each bone represents *one of the instruments of the passion of our Redeemer,* and the handler may lay out across the palm, a spear, the cross, the nails, and so on, and perhaps even place the little halo on their own head, or so a torn page from 1789 suggests it.

§

And then one filled with mermen and mermaids—various species of monkey attached by wire to the tail ends of fish.

§

And a much larger vault in which raining fish will be seen falling, every shower herein occurring from some of the first descriptions attributed to Phaenias of Eresus, and then to Phylarchus, and so of the fourth and third centuries before centuries began again, right through to the tiny fry of the Crucian Carp which fell frozen inside hailstones during a heavy storm at Essen in 1806, and the dozens of tiny red fish found on the roof of Mr. James McMaster's bungalow in Drumhirk in 1928.

§

And in another the exact same *remora*, or shark-sucker, which Pliny mentions, and this still attached to a fragment of the ship it delayed. That was the ship as Pliny records it, slowed by the drag of the foot-long fish on the prætorian hull. So well hindered was the galley indeed that the fish changed the fate of events at the battle of Actium. Or so those defeated were given to say. This would be nothing much in the scheme of things for a creature which *bridles the impetuous violence of the deep and subdues the frantic rage of the universe* merely by sticking itself to other things. It triumphs over the oceanic current by the most passive of all resistances. The head is secured with a cartilaginous disc by which it creates its suck, drawing the very same vacuum which nature is supposed to abhor.

§

And the so-called Emperor's Pike, hauled from a lake in Württemberg in the year 1497. It sported a copper ring about the gills upon which was found the insignia of Frederick II, who placed the thing in the lake in the year 1230. *I am the first fish placed in this lake by the ruler of the world in the year…* was how the inscription went. It so happened, nonetheless, that others recorded the same event but attributed the ring to a different Frederick, and with there having been so many Fredericks the age of the Pike came to vary considerably. Consequent of this, the wall contains the dried and over-varnished corpse of each and every Pike supposed to have been planted in a lake by a Frederick, although every single specimen measures nineteen feet and comes to a weight of five hundred and fifty pounds. Upon these particulars all accounts agree. For completeness— and the wall is nothing if not unabridged—the reputed skeleton of the Pike once preserved in the cathedral at Mannheim is also included, along with the report of a celebrated German anatomist declaring it had too many vertebrae, that is to say, it was a composite of multiple fish and had been lengthened to fit the story. So much for the skeleton at Mannheim.

—Hesiod is the originator of the ring-finding impulse, having claimed, so Pliny records, that a deer lives four times longer than a crow, and that a crow lives nine times longer than a man, which would place the life expectancy of the average stag to around two and a half thousand years. Rings were subsequently found on all manner of stags declaring their antiquity, some almost lost to sight in the grown over fat of the neck. Agathocles of Syracuse perhaps started it—his stag was tagged at Troy—and Charles VI of France, otherwise known as Charles the Mad was still doing it in the fifteenth century. HOC ME CAESAR DONAVIT, he said, look it reads HOC ME CAESAR DONAVIT, and so on.

§

And in yet another chamber will be found the very idea, suggested by Pliny, that the remora be attached to the bellies of *great bellied women* to *stayeth the dangerous flux of the womb* and thereby hold the child there til it reaches full term. *Remora*, in Latin, means delay backwards, or hinder—and so it stood to reason to suggest this course of action, thought those who did so. This idea is evidenced within the chamber not by the fragment of the manuscript in which Pliny makes his outlandish claim, but in the sound of every woman who has heard it suggested. These exclamations are produced by a contraption resembling a bellows.

§

THE LAND REMORA. He who talks and thereby bores another to death, or the feeling of drag produced by the talker, or the depressive sensation of downward pull exerted on the soul or its simulacrum, caused by an invisible yet ineradicable verbal chain. Or so Ben Jonson coined it.

§

The sucking-fish appears in multiple woodcuts from the sixteenth century, generally clasped along the keel, or at the side, or upon the rudder, and in league with other fishes and birds together bringing hell upon the crew. The sucking-fish appears also in *The Fourth Book of Pantagruel*, though merely in passing, now firmly displaced like most other creatures in that book by the greater mass of the King of Lent. Or by a verbal substitute for the King of Lent, who was almost but then decidedly not encountered on a sea voyage to the Oracle of the Holy Bottle. Given how the King of Lent is beyond description, Rabelais resorts to an enormous list of similes and a shorter one for metaphors, a list so long it makes its own futility apparent. No single allusion quite manages to attach itself firmly to the beast, and the accumulation of attempts gesture to that growing impossibility.

There is a room in the wall marked *Quarêmeprenant*, within which every failed allusion to the King of Lent will be found materialised, including *the left testicle of a male tick*—likened to the brain of the king, as well as a monocle for the tonsils, a turnip for the salivary gland, another turnip for the genitals, a harrow for the cheeks of the arse, a mustard pot for the colon, a padlock for the loins, a hundred tin tacks for the semen, a catapult for the bladder, a beggar's wallet for the marrow, a shoe-horn for judgement, a cushion-stool for reason, and tweakings of the nose for the vital spirits, alongside heaps and heaps of other sixteenth century objects, all of which are thrown about the chamber in a state of considerable disorder.

It might come as some surprise that the left testicle of the tick, a mere flick, should be found in all of that, although it will be less of a surprise to hear that I followed a tick into that place, and this is how I got there, and that is how I found the testicle, having come across the tick sometime earlier, a tick which happened to be in search of the thing, and so too was in search of the very idea that a tick, that the very tick before me, might have a testicle. The tick learned of the possibility from within one of the folds of reticulated skin upon the elephant, this fold containing, evidently, *The Fourth Book of Pantagruel*, lodged in the same recess as the tick.

The King of Lent is not there at all. Not one single solidary bit of him can be found in the entire chamber of sixteenth century objects once meant to locate or describe him. But the effect of it can still be sensed and will be felt as guilt travels, or as the sun leaves its day, for all surrounding chambers contain books that are voided as the King of Lent was absent, each book appearing, such as it could, without a single simile or metaphor included. These associations were either taken from those volumes by retraction—far too many books were all but destroyed in consequence—or the associations were absent because the texts never resorted to the practice of likening one thing to another in the first place. For his part, Rabelais reclaims the simile from its somewhat lazy work, from its often-easy manner of thinking, and to a lesser extent he does the same for the metaphor, showing how the practice can outdo and then ridicule itself by over doing. But this insurrection against two of the foremost tools of description will only be done once, before it too grows old and tiresome, like a joke retold.

§

The whale killed by Pantagruel is in the wall, much desiccated indeed, and again not far from the elephant, but outside the space of the voided simile. It was slayed by first gouging its eyes, and then by his filling it with arrows so that it came to look like a *three-master galleon, mortised and tenoned together by beams of the appropriate size, as if they were the ribs and channel boards of the keel*—a most pleasing sight, apparently—and after it turned over, coming to look like a hundred-legged serpent. This stuffed and dried relic has the peculiar characteristic of looking like different things from the same angle, rather than the more usual property of looking like different things—a ship, a serpent, the Cetus sent to devour Andromeda, and so on—from different sides and approaches.

§

Another ring was found by Roger Bacon in the thirteenth century, again from the time of Caesar and from the fat of the neck of another deer. Somewhat ruining the evidence, Bacon melted it down with a quantity of other brass objects, needing the lot for his brazen head, said to answer any question put to it.

—this might be the head I saw upon a pillar outside the elephant chamber, its mouth stuffed with brass rings, that is to say, with the evidence.

He left the region of the head, overcome by the brass rings that were not merely stuffed but welded into the mouth. And collided, as he did, with the objects and books that lay along the passageways, knowing it to be nothing, this knocking, for if he came back, or attempted to come back, he would see there could be no returning. These books would be recovered. Or some of these books would be recovered. And of those that were, the books would be positioned elsewhere when arranged for a different century. Some books absented entirely, yet others appearing for a first or subsequent time. The inner walls themselves reformulate after their shifting along and their breaking back, which is what they do without making dust or pains about it.

—even the most solid things here can be reduced to masticants—

The running itself was done as it has been done so many times before, a laughable kind of running from the outside, a bewildered, toilet pot style of locomotion. *He ran in his toilet pot way*, would be one way of writing it up, and perhaps a book would one day appear within the wall describing his toilet pot-like desperation. The same book might explain that the *toilet pot run* must not be mistaken for the run of the *chamber pot seeker*, which looks similar but is differently prepared, and should then delineate each of these from other near associates, such as the *latrine run,* or the run of *abject sensation*. For his part, he emerged from the wall to the original murmur of the flat with toilet pot haste. These are approximations, naturally, and he floundered for words when lying before the entrance to the wall, the dirt in his mouth clogging his tongue so it could hardly move and would not intimate a single letter. This too had been seen before, indeed there was nothing he did which had not.

§

Having left the wall this last time, he had an urge to dig himself a shallow pit to lie in, but found the ground of the flat too hard for that, and so crawled across it to where the infants lay exposed on the slopes to harden them off. There looking down at them the man took his beard, profusely grown, and wrapped it round a finger wondering, as he did so, if this might be considered a circumstantial detail. Still tied this way from chin to finger, the man knelt and then sat and then lay by the infants and looked with them to the heavens and moaned together at the leaden bowl.

§

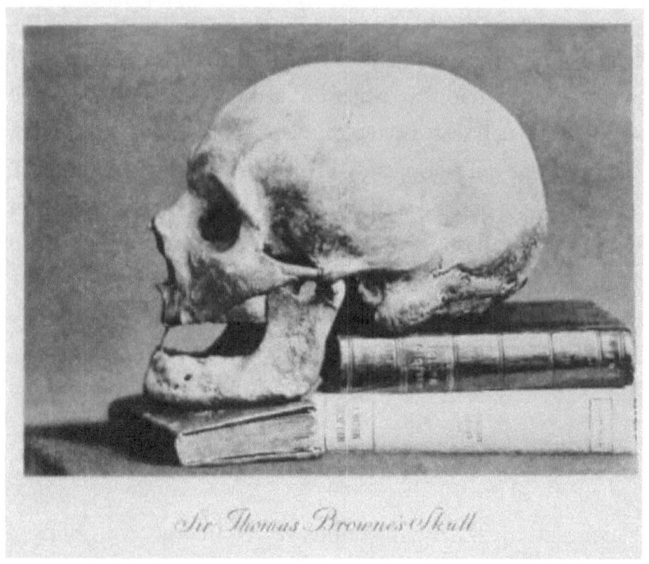

§

Thomas Browne LIES SLEEPING HERE is how the inscription runs, AND WITH THE DUST OF HIS BODY CONVERTS LEAD INTO GOLD. The date of his death is also listed, this being in the Year of Our Lord 1682.

When the coffin was hacked into or peeled open in the year 1840—entirely by accident the workmen claimed—it was still made of lead. Browne had liquified and subsequently dried out, though he had not yet become dust.

§

When the workmen dug in the chancel of a Norwich church, they came across a coffin made of lead and saw an opportunity. The sexton saw it too, which meant the opportunity became his. The casement was already dinted from their digging with a pickaxe and took only a little more persuasion to open like a tin of canned beef. The workmen knew of such things, having served in the navy where these eats were had. Tinned meats and other things sealed up in that manner had made it so far as the Arctic by now for one expedition or another, although this did not make canned goods commonplace, not yet, and the possible wit of remarking that Browne's coffin opened like a can of beef was not twenty or thirty years old owing to the comparatively recent invention of canning.

§

Here have we a part of Thomas Browne which even the man himself never saw, announced the sexton as he took the skull from the workmen, coveted it a bit, and then tried to hawk the thing to a Mr. Frith, who refused, and then to a certain Edward Lubbock, who became its possessor, although by the year 1845 this Dr. Lubbock had already had enough of it and deposited the skull in the pathological museum of Norfolk and Norwich Hospital. The sexton also took a handful of hair, described by somebody else, at another time some years later, as *profuse and perfect and of a fine auburn colour*, although it might have been the remains of a wig. The rest was brushed aside and remained along with the headless Browne alongside his new neighbour—the woman they were digging for—wife of the then incumbent Rev. John Bowman.

§

Browne's skull was removed from his coffin and sometimes looked at if not mainly shelved for sixty-two years until finally reburied in 1922. The vicar took some evident pleasure in recording *317 years* in the age column—the ink is unusually thick, and the calligraphy crude and over puffed—which made the entry of 80 years for Mary Ann Hawes, recorded in the row above, look rather measly.

§

Many curious objects were placed on hospital shelves, or inside curio cabinets, during the years 1840 to 1922, including Mary Bateman's pickled tongue in not-so-far-away Leeds. Alongside the skull, by the by, was a portion of Browne's beard, also not dust, and displayed in a glass vessel.

§

The man in the hole by the barrow held his own beard in one fist, or so I recall, and had Browne's book in the other, and said, look at my beard, and tell me it is not a wall. When he held his beard like that, the pull of it made his mouth smaller at one edge, and larger at the other.

§

When Browne's skull was delivered to the Norfolk and Norwich Hospital where it was shelved, and before copper ties were attached between the skull and mandible, otherwise known

as the *inferior third of the face*—to keep it from falling to the
position of a severe undercut, or to that of the head that has
fallen forward and struck itself by the chin—some fun was
had in making Browne talk, during which Browne's skull was
caused to say all manner of things, a range of situated witticisms
most probably, all of which were promptly lost to history. The
manner of their talking is known, however, in that they curled
their lips over their teeth to imitate Browne's toothlessness.
The alveolar ridges were thereby very well rendered, for merely
one single tooth socket remained, the rest being completely
absorbed and covered over.

§

Those manipulating Browne's skull did not quote him as they
might have done, and taste further, and more deeply, of the irony.

*—To be knav'd out of our graves, to have our sculs made drinking-
bowls, and our bones turned into Pipes, to delight and sport our
Enemies, are Tragicall abominations—*

Nor as they otherwise cavorted was fun had with the anecdote
of William Stukeley, which held that Browne *dyed after eating
too plentifully of a Venison Feast.*

§

Those messing with Browne's remains did indeed make his
skull say many things they thought very funny and all of these
things they made it say were exact and choice quotations from
his works.

There is another man within mee, they made it complain by clapping the mandible up and down, *another man that's angry with mee, rebukes, commands and dastards mee.*

—death hath spurs, and carcasses have been courted, was another.

§

When Browne's skull was placed atop a recently reissued collection of his works—this was 1904 or thereabouts—the gentleman placing it there took some pleasure in quoting the line—*but who knows the fate of his bones, or how often he is to be buried*—after which he returned to his earlier fixation, pressing the point that the image must look identical to the one inside the reissued collection. This image, its frontispiece, also depicted the skull laid on a pile of books. Would you like me to show you again, he asked, but the photographer declined, having seen it enough already.

Once the picture was taken, its photographer had to endure a longer quotation. This was directly read from the newly reissued collection and not told him from memory. It came from the book just then extracted from the base of the skull, the so-called still life, or volume II of it.

—men took a lasting adieu of their interred Friends, the man who commissioned the photograph went on, *little expecting the curiosity of future ages should comment upon their…* bones, he said, changing the text a little to suit the occasion.

The photographer collapsed his equipment, satisfied he had re-created the image within the reissued works which depicted the same skull, from the same angle, lit in the same way, but which was in that earlier photograph rump-rested upon a leather-bound volume of Browne's *Religio Medici*, and not *The Works of Sir Thomas Browne*, freshly pressed, pages uncut, just then sat there in his studio.

Subsequent onlookers when faced with the earlier photograph—the one which survives and not the re-staged photograph which does not—have taken similar pleasure in knowing and quoting that line, although what the pleasure and the satisfaction it trails exactly mean, or amounts to, is not clear. It could be the delicious irony of it all, with Browne now treated to what he once described—*look his skull has become just another relic like the Reliques he wrote of.* Although it is probably this and something more, a last and lasting yearning, a final need to see Browne's own inevitable submission to what he once described and then take reassurance from that inevitability. This closing wish from a time that is itself winding down. A desire from those living in that era to take it as a hopeful sign of THE INESCAPABLE POSSIBILITY OF BEING EXHUMED THEMSELVES, if buried, or picked over if reduced to ash—though not *pickled*, none would hope for that. This inescapable possibility is the reassurance, however unwittingly felt and if never fully articulated, of something universal issuing from that inevitability, the sensation of a continuous line of digging and being turned over, a civilizational troth, *the land will be dug,* if only to make foundations for new buildings, and that *the dead will be raised* and submitted to commentary, at least where they can be found. There is, in Browne's example, a surety of what survives of a person being turned between finger and thumb. This surety stretches forward from Browne's own living and Browne's own dying, reaching into the present, and so touches all those currently living—as they face their dying—just as Browne extended that line back to the ancients and so brought the very long dead back into the ambit of his discoursing. After so many centuries of damp quietude, the ash of each urn was exposed to the gentle ingress of Browne's extended hand and the protuberances of his reason, and was some of it unsettled, just as Browne's own corpse was shuffled about in that Norwich chancel, and then his cranium submitted to the grasping limb of each reader turning over to the frontispiece of the second volume of his collected works, and pausing there—for what—for this sensation. This is what lies behind the satisfaction of pointing out how Browne was reduced to a skull that did not know in advance but would now see how many times it could be buried. It is the satisfaction of thinking that Browne had himself buried in a lead coffin for what, for nothing, and then for something. And this something was unassailably material. He had himself laid as if he would rest, become bone, be borne upward, or till he was dust and would rise as dust rises only more gloriously. Here was how Browne had himself stored. His corporeal token was protected by lead from evil spirits coming from in the sides and up from below. His remains were to be carried in safety and without interruption to the day of Last Judgement. Yet even he, or precisely he, could not avoid becoming an artefact that other men would pick over, prefiguring as they did so, or perhaps profoundly supplanting the Last Judgement of the Book with all of the not so queasy, which is to say, far too easy judgement-making and column-filling of their epoch. His bones would endure beyond the memory of his friends and relations and travel far beyond the literal affections of any living person, and they would then thereafter stray into that stage bones reach whereafter digging them up, and making ornament of them, or indeed making a prop of them for the age of photography, is no longer evident desecration, or is a kind of desecration nobody would anymore shriek at but only rumble over. And if Browne is disturbed from his rest, from his doomsday waiting, at least this act of disturbance, this process of exhumation and inspection, this marking of pasts, of deaths, of the passing of centuries and civilizations, is some kind of historical constant, a treading-line that gives humankind some kind of consistency, a felt consistency, a constancy of outlook in spite of everything else which otherwise declares its fickle, insubstantial attentions. When the skull of Thomas Browne is placed upon a stack of books and looked at and remarked upon, or simply appreciated in its vacant reverie, this moment should not be underestimated as an ironic ploy, but will be deemed THE CURIOUS GIVING MOMENT OF CONJURED SUBSTANCES staged for an otherwise Godless, rudderless, and benighted humanity which may find its consistency if nowhere else in its continuity. Which is to say, in its capacity to bury itself over, and then bury itself over again.

§

The man in the hole by the barrow said things about Browne that anyone who knew anything about Browne would consider wrong, and as he said all this, made it possible for others to say things that were less wrong, but not so perfectly correct as they might have done.

§

He stood and looked outwards from the entrance to the wall. I will return to my city and gather the scent of mine own library, said he, and he would find a hollow of his own to live in, and from that hollow he would tell something of his travels.

§

I will return to my books, and the smell of them together, and from that together will select the one which reminds me of sausage meat.

§

Falling in with the belly folk he tried several of their shallow graves. I came across their hill slope early in my return journey, the man said from his barrow-side hollow.

§

Falling into the holes that the belly folk had for sleeping places, I knelt upon their sleeping bodies, said he.

§

Kneeling on sleeping bodies I came to see how it was I would learn to write of the softer things.

§

I left my travels and returned to the barrow, the man said, from which place he directed and misdirected all and any visitors.

§

I sent a note from the barrow, and this was my first deception. I myself was first deceived.

§

I sent a note that said I would return to the barrow, and this was the original deception after the first deception.

§

I sent a note that said I had come from the barrow, and this was the last lie, which made it superior to the original lie, and better even than the aboriginal lie.

§

I left the wall and climbed a ridge, the man said again. I climbed a ridge and found faces along it hard as clay. Each face had become something other than a living face even when resembling a face and told its truth with all manner of expression that living will not be paused.

§

I left the ridge and met a people who thought the sea to be higher than the shore and told these people of my wandering and they wrote it down, and it became part of the holy book.

§

He took Browne's book from my one hand, the younger man did, and was presented with a can of beef from out of the other. *Look at the rim,* I told him, *and tell me it does not look like a wall.*

§

He found a man living in a hollow surrounded by canned goods and at a greater radius by un-canned goods. Take the key of this one, he said, turn it about and remove the head of my tin for me and tell me this does not look like a wall.

§

A young girl bounded across the slope, and the man with the beard said, now look how I give her years in seconds.

§

I will tell you how the girl looked, he told me, and will tell you how she looked when sitting by the depths of that well, and still you will not see it. The man placed the girl there, at the well, and it was not seen just as said.

§

The man in the hollow placed people all over the earth, in all manner of positions, and all of it was not seen, as he proclaimed.

§

He would do whatever he pleased, raising a hammer at times to bash the sides of his pit. I can hammer here and there about and you will not hear it, he said to the onlooker, and the onlooker did not hear it.

§

I will tell you something, he told him then, something you cannot give ear to, at which point the listener bent over, and listened.

§

I will take you with me to the wall, said he, and you will not hear my feet or see me tread before you, and the follower did not know it or see him to be there.

§

I will hold every book I mention in the air, and I will defile its pages, and you will imagine them undefiled.

§

He took a book and bound it in human skin, and took a collapsible cup made of human leather and drank a toast to his book. I shall do this, and I shall tear out the hairs of my face, and yet still you will not vault off into the distance.

§

And I will write of the softer things and shall not tell you how I came to know them, and then I will cover the softer things with harder things and leave them on this slope.

§

And I will tell you what this woodcut depicts, and within its unregarded cavities I shall find future plans for this earth, and I shall see that it pinpoints with exactitude the time and place of as yet unrealised craters, and there will be cracks rent in the crust of the planet from quakes, and blizzards of ash, and lands overcome by fire and sand, and you shall not see them or know where to avoid their making.

§

I will describe the half-dug foundations of buildings that were themselves only half-planned and will lie fallow in their ironworks half-plundered, and you will not know how to avoid these wasted makings.

§

He took his finger in the palm of his other hand, and drew with that finger until it bled, knowing the blood he shed would never be tasted. I cannot bleed, he said, and you will only half believe it.

§

The troglodyte wet his lips, and that wetting made no sound, nor did it employ any wet.

He held a book, and this book could not exist, and reached up and out of the hole with it, and took this non-existent book and said, this is how books should be treated.

§

He took a non-existent book, and said, you will still imagine that this book exists, and you will see me as I drop it.

§

The book he held became another book, and that other book was also a non-existent book, and still it existed for a moment in the mind, to which the troglodyte laughed, and said, now see what I can do.

§

For why not be a little easy with the thought of such things, he thought, and why not contrive against them even when holding them, or precisely when holding them. And yet, there were books which remained outside his holding and beyond his retelling, and these were the books which stayed his hand and stayed his reading and his thinking. Browne stayed his hand, and so did Herodotus, although Herodotus also caused his hand to begin clawing, and with these claws it dug up Bateman, and having clawed at Bateman, clawed and dug against anything Bateman-like he could find.

§

He dug his way into the chancel at Norwich too, naturally, and rested himself between Browne and the priest's wife. He said it was better to lie between them before 1922, but not so close to 1840 or the first decades of liquefaction. He did return in 1924, and then again in 1939, but could not decide which pair of eyeless sockets he would rather stare into.

§

Having reached the top of the rise, I saw the man in his hollow.

§

Having followed the horse and its treading memory, I came across a half-dug pit with a figure inside.

§

Hearing the gate clap to, the man in the hollow sat up, and this when I first saw him. Every gate needs a hanging post and a clapping post, the man said upon seeing me, but my arm needs only its shoulder.

§

I found a post for the gate to clap to, and lowered it into the hole, only, a hand emerged, and then an arm, and finally a head, which said, my shoulder will be next.

§

I found a post for the gate to hang from, and lowered it into its hole, and when the hand emerged from this one too, I dropped it before there was another word said.

§

He hung the gate and clapped it shut, and said it would be a kissing gate, and that it would give way to the English Andes.

§

The gate was hung and the man was buried at last, and he saw that it was fitting given the circumstances for the man, who once lay in a hollow, to be in this space which was neither here nor there.

§

The fence was run along the side of the slope and a badger lumbered alongside the length of it with the uneven stride of its kind. And the badger ran, and the rains fell until the gate was lost, and the gap of it was filled, and the digging place passed over.

§

Walkers went through when the fence grew old and the wires of it came unlatched. And as their sticks gouged little holes, a finger or two came looking.

§

The fingers ceased looking, and the holes in the mud calloused over, and a herd of cattle came to live there. The earth was bespattered and pulped.

§

The cattle were turned off the land and some of their meat came to fill a little tin can that made its way to Argentina, or Patagonia, which seemed a good place to go and wait for things to end.

—he had wished to go to Patagonia and feel the last things before the last things stopped. Take me to Patagonia, he often said, and let me hear the world at the foot.

§

The land was lastly grazed by sheep, and these sheep kept it trim but for their matted hair. And the sheep were driven off, and the sky about their prints and sitting places fell upon the water.

§

The air was stagnant, the water brackish, and the earth black. There were no further murmurings, or nobody to heed them. It would have felt, if there were feeling left, that all things were coming to a halt, and nothing more would be done, and five thousand years had passed, and this would be it.

§

Having turned over in his hollow, the man nonetheless said there is no winding down, nor ending of a book, but merely the place where it is made to stop.

§

And he remarked, almost all books do end themselves, and close themselves in. And if there is a lamentable habit with the writing of a book, it is this demand to make the last words amount to a moment of completion, or resolution, or a falling off, or a coming to, or a rounding back, or whatever, so long as it seems fitting.

§

He said when he opened a book and read its first line, he could already feel the book preparing for its shutting off.

§

He said when he held a book, and placed the thing between his finger and thumb, he knew the book was superseded in that moment and by his holding of it, and the supersession would be done just as surely as the book was contained within his grasp. And that he found it perverse how so many writers and readers would find this a peculiar statement, which is how he came to live in his hole.

§

He said if he came to write a book, if he made the mistake of doing so, it would be all of it written, and then over-written, on the same disintegrating page.

§

He said that if he wrote a book, he would discharge himself into it, and make of it something nobody would wish to hold.

§

The man in the hollow held up the book, his non-existent book, and admired its thickness, and told me this, *I have herein achieved the longest palindrome in recorded history.*

§

The man in the hollow said that if a sentence is long enough and reads backwards as well as it reads forwards, that sentence will begin to embed itself in the earth, and shall be good for walking over, and will come to resemble the sign of eternity, and that it must form an orb eventually if sufficiently wound about and over itself, and even Empedocles would agree, and Anaximander would weep at the sight of it. By that sentence, which grows across time as it does across space, he would tread to all times and all places, and see the true futility of this mechanism they use to mark their having once been in the vicinity of a pen.

§

He said that he had written a book in the shape of an orb, and that he now held it in his gob.

§

The man in the hole remarked that if he wrote a book in the shape of an orb, he would roll it about until it gathered dust.

§

His visitor agreed that books usually gather dust on one or two surfaces, rather than all at once, and it made him sad.

He said that even now when he found dust laid thick along the upper pages of a book, it reminded him of a game he played with a friend who was now dead.

—they were young and bored, and looked for the least popular, or *the most pointless books* of the library they were stuck waiting in. The point was to take down those books which had not been taken out for years, and were not even browsed upon, and had been sitting completely undisturbed for the longest period, and then, wielding each his own choice hardback—for these cradled the most dust and effectuated the best launch—they took turns in blowing across the top. Each to see whose could fill the other's face with the worst pall. Nothing he tried with books in the years subsequent could match the pleasure.

END

ALSO BY ANSGAR ALLEN

Black Vellum

The Wake and the Manuscript

Plague Theatre

Burton's Anatomy

The Reading Room

The Reaches

The Sick List

Wretch

Cynicism

The Cynical Educator

Education and Philosophy

Benign Violence

BIO

Ansgar Allen is the author of books including *a short history of Cynicism*, and the novels, *Black Vellum, Plague Theatre, The Wake and the Manuscript, Wretch*, and *The Sick List*.

He is editor-in-chief at Erratum Press, and co-founded Risking Education, an imprint of Punctum Books. His writing has been published across a range of journals, books, and media, appearing in Chinese, Japanese, Spanish, German, Czech, Estonian, Farsi and Greek translation. He is based in Sheffield, UK.